# GET IN MY HEAD

## DANIEL'S STORY

S. M. HOLLAND

This novel is a work of fiction. Names, places, and incidents either are the product of the author's imagination or are used fictitiously. Any resemblance to actual persons, living or dead, events, or locations is entirely coincidental.



Cover art by Lia Bardin Bomar

Cover design by Poole Publishing Services LLC

To my Love,
For all those nights you stayed up with me as I checked the door locks on repeat, thank you for never once making me feel crazy. You always make me feel loved and important.

One. Two. Three. Four.

I tap my left foot on the soccer ball before I take a step back for the penalty shot. I glance at the rest of my team on the sidelines. Their ages range from fifteen to thirty-something. I can't miss this shot, or we'll tie and that's just as bad as losing. If we lose, I'll feel awful. If I feel awful, it'll be a shitty start to my senior year.

I can't miss. It's the last summer intramural soccer game.

I take a step back and let out a breath as my left foot makes contact with the ball. It snaps through the air just above the goalie's head.

"Yeah!" I yell and jump into the air as the rest of my team cheers and rushes toward me. We won!

The ref blows his whistle. "Redo."

"What? Why?" Jace blurts out and steps between me and the ref.

"Yes, why?" our coach asks. He's not that much older than me, so it's always funny to me to see him stand up to adults like this.

The ref points to the right corner of the field. Someone's kid was crawling towards the goal. "Distraction, the field is supposed to be clear. Whose kid is that?"

"Shit." One of the older guys from our team runs over to the kid and scoops her up. "I'm so sorry! I thought she was sleeping in her stroller."

"Redo. Clear the field."

Everyone walks back to the sidelines, their shoulders sagging. Crap.

No pressure. I pull in a deep breath and place the soccer ball back on the field. My heart races as electric shocks shoot down my arms and out of my fingertips. I tap them on my chest to stop the vibrations, then rub my sweaty palms on my shorts. A shiver runs down my spine. I would much rather wash my hands in the sink. With soap. I shake my head to get the thought to leave.

"One, two, three, four." The small crowd grows quiet as I rub my sweaty hands on my shorts again.

"You can do this, Daniel." I look over my shoulder to see Dad standing right next to Mom in the bleachers. A few others cheer out before falling quiet.

I tap my right foot on the soccer ball this time. One. Two. Three. Four. No, that didn't feel right. I try again with my other foot. One. Two. Three. Four. I shake my arms loose and take several steps back. I rush towards the ball, fake right, then go left. My foot makes contact with the ball and sends it sailing towards the upper right corner of the goal.

The goalie jumps up and the ball slides past one hand—

"Yea—"

But he manages to hit the ball away with the other hand.

The ground opens up below me and I sink to the bottom. An entire summer of games and we lose the whole season because of a penalty shot.

The other team rushes to the field, obviously grateful for the second chance, and hug their goalie. That's supposed to be us. Me. Instead, my team drags their feet, painfully slow, into the field to congratulate the other team.

"Hey man, no worries. That was cheap though. The ref favored the other team." Jace offers me his hand. "At least it's a tie."

I grab it and let him pull me up. "There goes all the good luck for my senior year."

"What? With that face? I don't think so."

The rest of the team makes their way over with their 'good season' and 'don't worry about it.' Along with the few who are blistering with anger over the ref.

I drag my feet over to my parents. "Hey, sweetie." Mom wraps her arms around me. I squeeze her back, but quickly let go. I'm sweaty and gross.

"You know, in my book, and everyone else's, you won that game," Dad says as he pushes me towards the direction of the exit.

"I agree. The ref's son was on the other team. He clearly had a favorite."

"Well, not much you can do with these intramural games I suppose. They're always hurting for refs," Dad says. We make it to the car. "You hungry?"

"I'm starving. But can I shower first?" I pull at the now-sticky jersey.

"We did bring your bag, just in case…" Mom offers. "You could shower here."

A chill runs down my spine as I imagine all the hundreds of other sweaty feet that have made contact with those showers. "Thanks, but can we go home first? Please?"

"Of course." She kisses my shoulder because she can't reach my cheeks anymore.

"Anything for you, Daniel. We're a team, remember?" Dad nudges me with his elbow before climbing into the front seat.

At least this is one team that will never leave me, even if I do screw up. I open up the door to the back seat.

"No, I'll sit back here. You can sit up front." Mom smiles and quickly slides in between me and the car.

"Don't you get car sick?"

"I'll be fine, it's not that far."

"Okay." I tap my fingers on my chest and pull in a deep breath before getting in on the other side of the car. Maybe that missed shot isn't a sign.

Maybe everything will be fine.

## September 1

I spent three hours at the mall with Mom this morning getting new clothes for school. I know it's frustrating for her, because I hate trying on clothes at the mall. But she would never tell me that. She'll make a big deal if she has to go back to return or exchange anything. Just to make sure I appreciate her and everything she does for me.

I do appreciate her. She does a lot for me.

-Daniel

I flip the lights on in my room as the sun disappears behind the rooftops across the street.

What am I wearing tomorrow? The orange polo? Maybe the blue one?

I glance over... better switch polos for tomorrow. The orange won't work with my shorts. After folding the polo back up, sharp corners, I place it neatly in my drawer. Then walk over to my bathroom and square off with the mirror and grab my toothbrush. Two minutes on the top. Two minutes on the bottom.

I tap the brush four times on the corner of the sink and place it in the mirror cabinet. My socks fly into the laundry basket, along with today's T-shirt, and I glance over to check that my backpack is ready for the first day of school.

Mom should be coming up any second to say goodnight on her way to bed.

I get up to re-stack my school clothes on my desk for tomorrow and notice creaking in the hallway. Must be Mom now.

"Goodnight!" I call out, trying to be heard but not be too loud. When no one answers, I walk out into the hall to wish Mom goodnight. Instead of Mom, I find Dad walking down the stairs with an extra blanket.

Something's wrong. "Dad?"

"Oh, hey." Apparently lost for words, the silence carries from his mouth. Finally, he says, "Just grabbing an extra blanket from the guest bedroom. It's getting a bit chilly downstairs. What time you waking up in the morning?"

Why didn't he just grab another blanket out of his bedroom closet? "Uhh. Six."

"Oh. See you in the morning then." And with that he turns and continues down the stairs, blanket held tightly to his chest.

**September 2**

First day of school today. I woke up to a text from Kayla. It's been hard to keep in touch with her this summer. The internet seems to be spotty over in Pakistan, and her dad's family has been keeping them really busy. I can't wait to see her. And to kiss her.

I got voted in as soccer captain this summer, with Garrett as my co-captain, and I'm this year's student body president. The one thing that would make this year even more perfect would be Kayla and Garrett finally getting along. Being stuck in the middle of their hatefest sucks.

-Daniel

Before heading downstairs for breakfast, I look around my room. The books on my bookshelf are lined up from tallest to shortest. My bedspread is pulled tightly over my mattress. I blink my eyes tightly four times, then knock my knuckles on the top of my desk six times, two knocks at a time before standing up tall and stretching out my spine. Walking over to my bedroom door, I tap the doorknob four times, punching in the lock after each turn. It's going to be a good day.

I pause before opening the door, straightening out my T-shirt and checking everything twice. I grab my backpack and try to make sure everything is done in the right order. I open the door and close it softly behind me, placing an open palm in the center of my door. For the first time this morning, I take in a deep breath. Now I'm ready for my day. I let out a sigh of relief and turn around to head downstairs.

When I reach the bottom of the stairs, I skip the bottom step and drop my bag on it. Right. I'm starving. Before I can make it into the kitchen, the office door cracks open. Dad, with eyes half-closed steps out in a T-shirt and boxer shorts, holding a pillow and blanket to his chest. What is he doing? I stand in silence and watch as he sneaks around the corner.

My heart speeds up. Is something wrong? Shit, did I do something wrong? Is he avoiding me?

I race back up the stairs just as their bedroom door closes and rush back into my room. My palms begin to sweat. I lunge into the bathroom and wash my hands. Four pumps of soap, scrub for sixty-four seconds, rinse for just as long. I shake my hands over the sink and let them air dry for a moment. I can't remember how clean the hand towel is, so I pick a new one.

I look around my room again, my books still in their place, tallest to shortest across the two long bookshelves built into the wall. My bed, made, the top blanket pulled as tightly as I could get it across the mattress. Everything is in place. I blink my eyes tightly four times, then knock on my dresser, six times, in sets of two. I stretch out my spine and stand tall, shoulders back. Next, I walk over to my bedroom door and tap the doorknob four times, punching in the lock each time. I straighten out my shirt and open my bedroom door, closing it softly behind me after I step out, and place my hand in the center of the door.

Let's try this again. I will my heart to stop racing and rush down the stairs, skipping the bottom step.

"Daniel, you're going to be late for school," Mom calls from the kitchen.

"Sorry." I sit down on a stool in front of the kitchen counter and stare at my plate of eggs and toast. "It smells good. Thank you." I reach for a fork, but hesitate for a moment.

"What's wrong?" Mom leans over the counter and rests her elbows on the cool marble.

"Nothing. I mean, something... But, never mind." I tap my fingers over my heart counting to four with each finger beat over my sternum. Mom taught me to do this when I was little and I couldn't control my feelings or impulses. She said it was a good way to help center me. I've been doing it ever since. Sometimes I don't even realize I'm doing it.

"Your OCD is showing." Mom winks and gets up to pour herself a cup of coffee.

"I'm pretty sure you can't say things like that." I place each hand palm down on either side of my plate before grabbing my fork.

"Well—sorry. What's bothering you?"

I shake my head and take a bite of eggs before cutting a slice of jellied toast with the side of my fork.

"You know toast is considered finger food, right?" Her love language is sarcasm.

"Why did Dad sleep in the office last night?" I shove a piece of toast in my mouth with my fork.

"Oh? Yes. Well, I was having trouble sleeping, and he was kind enough to let me have the bed." She forces a smile and walks over to the fridge. "Do you want some coffee?"

"No." I shake my head. Part of me doesn't believe her. She stiffens, like someone shoved a rod through her body starting at the top of her head. She's definitely lying. Maybe I messed up this morning? Maybe I forgot a step? I squeeze my eyes as I go over all the steps of my morning ritual.

I didn't forget anything. Maybe it's stopped working? My heart migrates to my throat.

"Good morning!" Dad grabs the tops of my shoulders and gives them a squeeze. "Your car's still in the shop, so one of us will have to take you to school."

"I can take my bike. Thanks, though." I square my shoulders and shove another bite into my mouth. He's too enthusiastic this morning. Overcompensating?

"You sure? We're on your team. Your mom and I have to be on that side of town anyways."

"For what?" I ask.

Mom clears her throat and shoots Dad a glare. "Just running some errands."

Dad nods.

My fingers go up to my chest again and I tap on my sternum.

"Are you ready for your senior year? Principal Johnson said you're the predicted valedictorian. It's between you and some girl named Shayla Jacobsen? But we have faith in you Mr. Student Body President! You're going to knock it out of the park this year." He rubs my shoulders again before wandering over to the coffee pot.

He and Mom avoid each other. Must have been some fight last night for them to not want to even look at each other.

"Thanks, but I should get going." I stand up and place both hands on either side of my plate before grabbing my backpack at the bottom of the stairs and my pre-packed soccer bag by the front door. "I'm going to be late." I tap the doorknob four times before opening it. Being late on the first day of school is bad luck.

**September 5**

The first few days of school have been amazing. Everything has returned back to normal after the summer. We had our first student body meeting yesterday, and clubs start next month.

Kayla is still as perfect as ever. I don't know how I ever got so lucky to have her. Yeah, that's mushy, but I want to remember this year. My last year of high school is going to be one for the books.

At least things are good at school. It's time to get to the bottom of the weirdness at home. Maybe Dad insulted one of Mom's paintings again. The last time he made a comment about one of her commissioned pieces, she gave him the silent treatment for a week. She's funny like that. But Dad always deals.

-Daniel

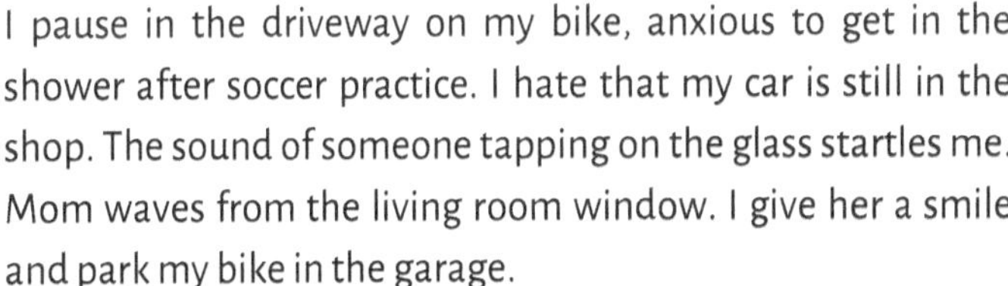

I pause in the driveway on my bike, anxious to get in the shower after soccer practice. I hate that my car is still in the shop. The sound of someone tapping on the glass startles me. Mom waves from the living room window. I give her a smile and park my bike in the garage.

Dad opens the door for me. "Hey, your mom and I want to talk to you. Come have a seat." His voice is tight and shallow.

Did someone die? "Can I shower first?" I pull at my gym shirt.

"After we talk to you, sweetheart." Mom pats the cushion next to her.

"But I'm gross."

"Please."

My skin itches as sweat and dirt begin to dry all over my body. I clench and open my hands before taking a deep breath. Goosebumps spread over my arms and legs. They're both acting weird. Is this about their fight? Maybe they're apologizing?

I sit next to Mom on the very edge of the couch as Dad sits in his favorite chair across from us.

Tension hangs in the air, making it difficult to take in a deep breath. Dad clears his throat and stares at the carpet. The sweat and dirt left on my skin from soccer practice feel like fire ants crawling all over my body.

Mom starts to speak, "Dan—"

"I need to shower." I jump up as Mom grabs my arm.

"Can't that wait? We really need to talk to you—"

"After I shower. I'm gross, I need to be clean."

"Daniel." Dad's voice is low and sad.

I sit back down and Mom grabs my hand. I watch as the germs travel from my skin and consume her.

"Your dad and I have been struggling for a long time," she begins. "We don't connect anymore—"

"Counseling—are you going to counseling?" I cut her off. Whatever it is, it can be fixed—I can help fix it.

"Yes, we went to counseling. That was the first thing we did when we didn't fit together anymore."

Didn't fit? Like they're a damn puzzle?

"Daniel," Dad speaks up, "Your mom and I are—"

"Don't," I beg. "Please, we can work on this together, you haven't let me help yet—"

"It's not yours to fix." Dad moves from his chair and sits on the other side of me and rubs my shoulder leaving my other side feeling empty and hollow, where Mom sits, drying her tears with her sleeve. "Your mom and I are getting a divorce."

He's going to leave me. I'm going to be all alone. Mom's going to check out and I'm going to get abandoned—left behind. Isn't that how the story goes? Thousands of tiny needles burrow their way into my body, leaving me cold and numb. I reach up and squeeze my other shoulder, hoping it would help me warm up. I don't know why, I don't think I'll ever be warm again.

"This has nothing to do with you, or how we feel about you, Daniel. Your dad and I still love you very much." A sob slips out of Mom.

"Your mother's right, we still love you. We know this is going to be difficult."

"No one is moving anywhere until after you graduate, though. We thought it would be better if we tried to keep some sense of normalcy until you go off to college."

"We didn't want you to keep wondering why we've been sleeping in different rooms."

"Been sleeping? How long have you been sleeping in different rooms?" I ask, but I'm not sure I want to know.

Mom and Dad look at each other, then at the floor.

"Since April," Dad says.

Shit. "When did you decide you would be getting a divorce then?"

"August."

"Why didn't you tell me then?"

"Honestly, we were trying to keep everything under wraps

until after graduation. But then you saw your dad sleeping in the office, and I couldn't lie to you anymore," Mom replies.

"We... we couldn't lie to you anymore," Dad adds.

My stomach hurts. Not the normal, I-ate-something-bad stomachache but the hollow, thick, I'm-going-to-die feeling. "I, um. Can I go shower now? Please?" My heart slams itself into my spine, then back into my sternum.

Mom nods.

"Sure, Daniel. If you have any questions, ask. Your mom and I are open books from here on out." Dad blinks rapidly and clears his throat.

I run up the stairs, through my room, straight into my bathroom and turn the shower on as hot as it will go, then slam the door closed. I roll up my clothes and place them in the hamper and jump in the shower before the dam breaks. My tears mingle with the stream from the showerhead. Sob after sob racks my body.

This can't be happening. Things like this don't happen to my family. We always work through stuff together. We are a team.

All those years of them telling me that we were a team feel like shit now. Like the dirt rinsing off my legs and swirling down the drain. I grab my scrub brush and dump way too much soap on the bristles, even for my standards, and scrub the dirt and sweat off with as much force I can muster. I don't stop until I feel clean, not just my skin, but my insides, my mind. I scrub until the hurt and the anger fade and get replaced with a dull aching headache and raw skin instead.

## September 6

Today I woke up in hell. I had a dream last night that my parents were pulling the shittiest practical joke on me. But I woke up to see Dad leaving the office again. This time he left the pillow and blanket on the couch. I couldn't handle it. I had to fold up the blanket and put everything away in the linen closet. Maybe if I help keep the chaos in order, everyone will be less stressed, and my parents can work this mess out better.

-Daniel

---

"Hey, wait up." Garrett grabs my shoulder and turns me around. The pressure on my left side has made the right side feel unbalanced.

"Hey." I reach up and squeeze the top of my right shoulder to try to balance out the pressure.

"Dude, you okay? We've hardly hung out since Kayla returned, and you just walked past me like I wasn't there. What's up?"

I shake my head. "Nothing." And head towards my first class.

"Is it Kayla? She finally dump you?" Garrett tries to hide a smirk.

"No. I know you've never liked her, but you don't have to blame her every time I'm in a mood."

"Not blaming. Hoping, maybe, but not blaming."

I roll my eyes and step around him. "You're going to make me late."

"I don't care."

I step around him again and he steps in front of me again. "Look, you can't just brush me off like that. Talk to me." He shoves my shoulder after I don't respond. "Come on, man!"

The strange hollow feeling returns to the opposite side of my body, screaming to be balanced out like a fire waiting to be quenched. I clench my jaw and grip the strap on my backpack with both hands until my knuckles turn white.

He doesn't have the right to treat me like this. Or her. I have always been there for him. He can give me a break. I ignore him and keep walking to class. The bell is about to ring, the halls are already empty.

"Come on—" Garrett grabs me again.

"I'm going to be late!" I snap.

"I don't care!" He goes to reach for me again—

"Boys!" Principal Johnson's voice echoes down the hall.

Garrett shoves me into a locker as the final bell rings. "Why do you have to be such an asshole? *Asshole.*"

"You don't know what you're talking about." I shove him back. "That's for letting Kayla's name come out of your mouth."

"You should be more worried about what's been going in her mouth."

"Garrett Hunter, Daniel Quincy! Mrs. Lewis' office, now! I'm calling to let her know you're on the way," Principal Johnson shouts.

Dammit.

Garrett follows me down the hall and around the corner to the counselor's office, huffing and puffing the whole way. He tosses his bag on the floor. I keep mine on my back and take a seat in one of the two chairs in the small waiting room.

"Boys, Mrs. Lewis will see you two in a minute. She has someone on the way to see her right now from the main office," the secretary says after he picks up the phone. He mumbles something else into the receiver before dropping the phone into its cradle and flashing us a knowing smile.

"Daniel." Garrett sits beside me.

I clear my throat and press my arms to my sides, lightly bumping my elbows on the armrests of the chair until the pressure feels even. We sit in silence for several moments. The wall clock ticks away, slowly getting louder as the sound takes over my senses.

I count them in my head. One…Two…Three…Four…

"Hi, I—a, um, am supposed to be seeing the guidance counselor." A blonde girl walks into the office and up to the desk, breaking the heavy silence between Garrett and me.

"Well welcome, welcome!" Mr. Commerce stands up from behind his desk and grabs a piece of paper from her. "Nice to meet you Sara, go ahead and have a seat and we will get you taken care of in a few minutes." He smiles before walking out of the office.

She turns around and I avert my eyes. It's embarrassing enough to be here instead of in class. I'm sure she's assuming the worst about me already. I clear my throat again and squeeze my arms tighter around my middle. She moves to the corner and leans her back to the wall. This office is really small.

"You can sit here." Garrett jumps up and offers his seat to the girl.

"Oh, no, that's okay. I can stand," she protests.

"I insist!" He waves his arms like a game show host.

After a couple long awkward moments, she pulls the chair

closer to the wall opposite me and takes a seat.

"So, you got in trouble or something?" Garrett asks as he leans on an empty desk.

"What? No. Just moved here."

"Really? Where are you from?"

"Uh, well, I don't know how to answer that question." She awkwardly looks at the floor and shifts in her seat.

"Witness protection? Yes! Did you hear that, Daniel? This chick is undercover!" He lets out a laugh that rattles the windowpanes.

"Ha. Sorry about him. He gets excited over little things. Like shiny objects. Or squirrels." Or me. He couldn't leave me alone so I could get to class. "I'm Daniel."

"Nice to meet you, Daniel, I'm Sara." She sticks out her hand, like she's about to sign a business contract with me. I'm really not up for any more human contact... maybe she'll put it down.

"I'm Garrett!" Garrett grabs her hand, over-enthusiastically. Well, at least he's good for breaking the standoff. "Nice to meet you, girl-who-doesn't-know-where-she's-from."

"Yes. Uh, thanks. I think?" She pulls her hand out of his.

What's taking Mrs. Lewis so long? I need to get this punishment meeting over so I can get back to class. I've missed too many notes... I'll fall behind...

"How can you not know where you're from?" My voice cracks in the middle as I rub the tops of my knees.

"My dad's in the military. I've probably moved about a hundred thousand times before now."

"Yeah, we get some of those military brats here now and again," Garrett jumps in. Great. Maybe he'll talk to her and I can be the first into the office. And first out.

Instead of taking the opportunity, I blurt out, "Why are you starting classes late?"

"My dad just deployed, then I was sick. My brother's started already, though. Not that you would care. I mean you might care, but I don't see why you would." She turns a little red in the face.

"How many brothers do you have?"

"Three. One's in college, one's my twin, and one younger, he's a freshman. I'm a junior, and my other brother is a junior too. Of course he is, because… of the twin thing…" She grabs her stub of a ponytail.

"Sara?" Mrs. Lewis walks out of her office and smiles. "Come on back, I have your class schedule."

"Thank goodness! Um, I mean, it was great meeting you guys. Bye." She stumbles a bit on the way up, and Garrett snickers. I elbow him in the side before she notices. Then knock my other elbow into the chair.

I rub my elbows and pretend that it doesn't hurt. "Look, I'm sorry. I'm just really stressed."

Garrett shrugs, his smile drops into a frown. "Yeah, just forget about it. It's okay." After several moments of silence, his smile returns. "That new girl though, she's cute." "Did you see how red she got? I feel bad for her. I think I would die if everyone always knew when I was really embarrassed." At least, I hope no one can tell.

"I think it's adorable. I would follow her around all day just to see her glow."

"Maybe you should ask her out."

"With her three brothers and a military dad? No fucking way, dude. I will just admire her glow from a distance."

"So you're going straight into the fire?"

"Like a moth to a flame."

We burst out in laughter before the office secretary walks back in and shushes us.

Silence fills the room again as we await our punishment.

## September 8

I was late for homeroom this morning. It was stupid. I woke up really early to shower and clean my room, because I always feel really good leaving a clean space. I've been so busy with school and soccer that I had neglected my room. It hit me out of nowhere how messy everything was. I started out dusting my desk and then all of a sudden I felt trapped and couldn't leave my room until it was done.

I might still be in my room now if Dad hadn't walked in with some laundry to put away. He was working from home today doing paperwork instead of at the clinic and didn't even know I was still there. I feel really stupid about it. I may have also had a small panic attack as he pushed me out the front door.

-Daniel

## September 15

It's almost midnight, and my parents are wide awake, whisper-yelling at each other downstairs. I don't think they realize I can hear them. I've never heard them have a major argument before, let alone yell at each other. I mean, maybe a few times over Mom's paintings, but that's something I've grown used to; they're never that big of a deal.

I've been arranging the pens and markers in my desk drawer, this time in sets of eight, every eighth one being blue. I want it to help me feel better, despite the silent World War III going on in my living room. Instead, every time I'm almost done arranging, the few missing pieces left remind me that some things just can't be arranged. I threw the pens that don't fit in the trash. I threw them too hard, and they scattered off the rim around the room. I wonder... how much stuff do I have to throw away to make things fit again?

-Daniel

## September 21

I think there's something wrong with me. My heart races at random times and I can't seem to catch myself. My parents are arguing more, less quietly now. They said they would stay under the same roof until I left for college. Maybe I'm not helping them out around the house enough? I don't know what else to do. I have to fix it.

-Daniel

———

"Hey, Daniel? Are you in there? Your dad said I could come up, I hope that's okay?" Kayla knocks at the door again.

I lay in my bed, drenched in my own sweat. I know I'm being dramatic, but the more my parents argue, the more disgusted I am with myself for not being able to hold it together.

"Did you forget we have a date tonight? Daniel? I'm coming in—"

"No!" I grab my face and try to breathe. My heart is racing a million miles an hour. The only thing that is helping me stay focused is biting the inside of my lip. "Don't come in."

"Are you all right? I can help, Daniel. Please let me come in." She sounds more sad than frustrated.

"Just—no. I'm fine. Just meet me downstairs, please? I'll be down in a few minutes."

"Are you sure?"

"Yes. Go." I hear her walking down the stairs and I try to regain my composure. One, two, three, four. One, two, three, four. One, two, three, four. One, two, three, four. Tapping on my sternum the whole time.

I jump in the shower instead, hoping it'll help calm me down. I close my eyes and the hot water runs over my face.

I lost track of time. After going through my ritual that is normally reserved for mornings, I run downstairs, skipping the bottom step and rush into the living room. Kayla sits on the edge of the couch alone, visibly annoyed.

"Hey, I didn't know a few minutes meant forty-five. Your dad isn't exactly the most entertaining human on the planet." Kayla's sarcastic tone makes me wonder if she hates me now.

"I'm sorry. I just really needed to take a shower." I grab her hand as we walk out the front door.

"So you did forget." She leans into my shoulder and the hairs stand up on the back of my neck. I'm trying really hard not to let go of her hand to squeeze my opposite shoulder to balance out the pressure.

"Where do you want to go?"

"A bunch of our friends are hanging out at the bowling alley tonight, do you want to go there?"

"Won't there be a lot of people there? We won't really get to talk."

"It has been a while since we hung out with all our friends together. I really want to go. I've been gone all summer surrounded by a billion family members who don't speak English. I want to hang out with my friends."

"Sure, yeah. You're right."

I open the car door for her, and we drive the short distance to the bowling alley. But I can't get out of the car. How often do they clean the bowling balls? Like thoroughly clean them? I picture someone who just licked their fingers shove them into the holes of a bowling ball and shiver. I open up the center console to grab my hand sanitizer. Gone. How long has it been out? I rub my sweaty palms across my thighs.

"Are you sure you're okay, Daniel?" Kayla asks.

"No. Yes. I don't know." One, two, three, four. One, two, three, four. One, two—

"It'll be fun. Just come in and say hi, and if you're still not feeling it, we can go."

"Promise?"

"I promise."

I continue to sit there, tapping my fingers on my chest. One, two, three, four.

"Ready?" Kayla asks.

"Oh. You mean I need to get out of the car?" I laugh, trying to break the tension that has quickly filled up the small space.

"That would be a good first step." She opens her door and gets out.

Okay, I can do this. They're my friends. Dammit, did I forget to turn my sink off?

Kayla gets back in the car and plops down in the seat.

"Let's leave, Daniel." She closes the car door and buckles back up.

"No, no you want to hang out with your friends. We should go in."

"This is stressing you out. I shouldn't be pushing you."

I let out a sigh and turn the engine back on. We sit in silence for several minutes as my heart races in my throat and I tap the steering wheel. Four times on one side. Four times on the other. But the steering wheel isn't lined up straight, so it still doesn't feel right.

"So... This is everything I hoped our first date after the long summer break would be." Kayla crosses her arms over her chest.

"I need to tell you something."

"Well, you're holding me hostage, so shoot."

I roll my eyes, "I'm not holding you—never mind." I swallow hard and clench my jaw for a moment. Please don't cry. You'll look like an idiot. "My parents are getting a divorce. They said they're going to keep living together until graduation—you know, like roommates or something. To try and keep things 'normal' or whatever."

"Oh my gosh! Daniel!" She unbuckles and flings her arms around my neck. "Why didn't you tell me sooner?"

I shrug. I hate saying it out loud.

"How are you dealing with all of this? Are you okay? Who all knows? Is that why you've acting all weird?"

"You, no one else knows."

Her grip loosens. "Not even Garrett?"

I shake my head as I catch a quick smile slide off her face. It's always a competition with those two. "I'm sorry, I don't think I can handle being around everyone right now. I'm too stressed out."

"Don't be sorry. I should be sorry. I knew something was off." She kisses my cheek. "That's so terrible about your parents.

Let's go through a drive-through or something, then we can park and talk."

"You sure?" I look over at her and my heart sinks. She shouldn't have to put up with me and all the shit that's happening in my life right now.

"I'm sure." She buckles up. "You need a chocolate milkshake and fries."

"Yeah." I smile a little as my heart slows down. "That sounds really good."

## September 30

Last night I couldn't sleep, so I cleaned the kitchen and living room. I woke Mom up, but instead of her telling me to go to bed, she joined me and we ended up mopping floors and dusting shelves together. It made me feel better. Maybe if I help out more around the house, Mom and Dad would be less stressed and they could work things out.

I feel better after everything's been cleaned, and stays clean. Maybe if they see I'm really trying, they'll try harder too.

-Daniel

"Hey, jerkwad. Why didn't I get invited to bowling?" Garrett closes my locker in front of me and winks before lightly punching me in the arm.

I swing my bag around so it bumps into my other arm. "Because you never pay for your own shoes. Or bring socks," I respond.

Garrett's eyes light up as soon as a couple of girls walk past us and drops the conversation as soon as it starts. "Hey, New Girl. Remember me? From the guidance counselor's office?" He smiles and steps in front of the blonde we met in Mrs. Lewis' office.

"Um. Yeah. Hi." She closes her locker.

"So how are you liking this school so far?" Garrett steps closer.

It didn't turn out well last time he tried flirting with this girl, so why is he trying again? The bell is about to ring.

"Okay, I guess." Sara takes a step back.

"Garrett, she's clearly not interested in you, can we go?" I tap my fingers on my leg as I resist the urge to pull him back.

"Is that true, New Girl? Am I creeping you out?" Garrett asks.

"Uh…" She looks anxious.

Did the bell ring? We're going to be late.

"You creep everyone out, now lay off." Lauren, the girl next to Sara, is loud and confident. She sets her dark eyes in a steely gaze, ready to take on anyone who questions her.

"Aw, come on, you always ruin all my fun." Garrett produces an exaggerated pout.

"You should have listened to Daniel, he was trying to spare you any more humiliation." Lauren flips her hair.

"I'm talking to the new girl, not you and your loud mouth. You can keep walking to class." Garrett plasters a smug smile across his face.

"Oh, I am walking to class. With my friend, Sara. She has a name you know."

Why hasn't the bell rung?

"What if she wants to walk with me? I am way more adorable than you." Garrett grins.

"We're not even going to the same class." He is always making me late.

"So. New Girl, come on, this is no competition. Who do you think is cuter? My awesome self? Or, her…" Garrett nods towards Lauren.

"Lauren," Sara blurts out.

"Well shit. You're batting for the other team. That's okay. I dig it."

"No! I'm not—I—" She blushes.

"So what, don't be jealous," Lauren says and grabs Sara by the arm.

"You embarrassed her." I elbow Garrett. He ignores me.

"It is adorable how easily you turn red, New Girl."

"You're an asshole." Lauren links arms with Sara. "And wouldn't you like to know what team she's on? I guess you will never find out. Because you're an asshole. Assholes don't get such privileges."

"Hey, I am a patient guy. I can wait. All day."

"You're going to have to wait longer than that, dude."

"Dammit."

Lauren and Sara turn away together. "Bye, Daniel!" Lauren waves.

"Bye."

"Hey, no sayonara for me?" Garrett shouts.

"Not in a million years!" Sara shouts back.

"Ha! She can speak!"

"Hey," is all I can say. Garrett finally looks at me, and I become very aware that I'm tapping the locker and my elbow in rhythms of fours. I put my hands down. I really need to get to class.

I turn and say to Garrett behind me, "I'm going to wash my hands."

"What? You just washed them a minute ago, are you okay?"

"Yeah, then I touched that stupid locker while you were flirting with Sara again." I start running to the bathroom before Garrett can argue. Then the bell rings. One, two, three, four.

## October 1

When I was little, Mom used to count to four with me to help me calm down. I used to have panic attacks all the time. I think I'm having them again. Air gets ripped out of my lungs at random times, over the stupidest things. Then I feel like an idiot for not being able to calm myself down again.

As a child it made me feel confused, and now it makes me angry. How hard can it be to keep myself calmed down and under control? Why does it always have to be such a battle?

-Daniel

———

I lean my head against the inside of my locker. Was I picking up my math book or dropping it off? One, two, three, four. One, two, three, four. One, two, three, four. I try to take in deep breaths as I tap my fingers on my chest one at a time. One, two, three, four. One, two, three, four.

"Hey are you okay?" Garrett walks up behind me.

"No—no. Stop." I have to start over. "One, two, three, four. One, two, three, fo—"

"Daniel, what are you doing?" He grabs my arm and my stomach instantly churns.

It feels as if a hummingbird is buzzing between my ears as sweat drips down my temple.

"Seriously Daniel, you're acting really weird."

"I'm sorry—I'm sorry. I need to go." I try to walk away but he won't let go of my arm.

"Just tell me."

A frustrated sigh escapes my lungs and I quickly clench my jaw shut. "My parents are getting a divorce." My skin crawls before I can finish the sentence.

"Oh." He stares at me, still holding firm onto my arm. "Wow. I'm really sorry. Shit, that's fucked up. But hey, it's not that big of a deal, parents get divorced all the time."

Of course he would say that. Does he even remember his parents being married? They've been divorced for as long as I've known him. How could he understand? This isn't supposed to happen to my family. My family has always been a team. This isn't normal. It's not supposed to happen to me.

"I—I need to go—please let go." He drops my arm. I tap my fingers on my chest faster and keep walking, leaving Garrett standing alone in the hallway looking at me like I'm a two-headed freak.

The second I get around a corner, I run to the closest restroom and close the door behind me before the final warning bell rings for the next class period. I turn the sink on full blast and wash my hands until my heart stops pounding so hard in my chest.

"Shit." I breathe out. I left my math book in my locker. I turn to grab a paper towel, only to see the dispenser is out. Of course it is. I slowly turn the faucet off with the side of my hand instead, and avoid the automatic hand dryer. I shiver thinking about the germs they blow out. After shaking the excess water off my hands, I hurry to the door and freeze. I walked into the wrong restroom. It's the one that pulls in, not pushes out. My heart slams into my sternum, reminding me that I'm already late to class.

I look at the door handle again as it stares back at me and

clench my fists at my sides. This is so stupid. Just open the door. I push all the germy thoughts from my head and reach for the handle. The door swings open before I can touch it.

"Oh, sorry—" Jace walks in and nearly bumps into me.

"Thanks!" I rush out before he can say anything else and jog to my locker, which was left open, and find a note on top of my math book.

*'Hey, we really need to talk. You are stressing me out.*
*I'm sorry about your parents.'*

-Garrett

I crumple the note and throw it into the back of my locker, but quickly change my mind and straighten it out and shove it into my math book. I don't need this right now. I suck in a few deep breaths and count to four several times to calm myself down before finally heading to class.

Late.

The few seconds of calm leave as quickly as they came, and my heart pounds faster and faster the closer I get to class.

## October 2

The parents are gone and Kayla is coming over tonight. It feels like forever since Kayla and I have been alone together. I still haven't made up for keeping her from bowling with her friends. I've also vacuumed and dusted my room four times and re-straightened all my books. I know it's stupid and unnecessary, but I feel like I have to do it. I'll get over it. I'll get over it. I'll get over it. I'll get over it. And of course I had to write that down four times.

What the hell.

-Daniel

"Are you sure your parents are going to be out for a while?" Kayla closes my bedroom door, runs over, and jumps on my bed.

"Yeah, I'm sure. They both left in different cars, for 'alone' time. Whatever the hell that is. They both told me separately they would be really late. My mom even said she might not be back tonight." My stomach sinks at the thought. Is she going to leave me?

"Kiss me." Kayla leans in and grabs my face, her lips meeting mine. I push her away.

"Wait, I want to wash my hands."

She lets out a huff. "You're lucky that I like you so much, or all your random germaphobe stuff would really get to me."

"I am very lucky." I run to my bathroom really quick and wash my hands. Then I brush my teeth. I wash my hands again. Run my fingers through my hair, and wash my hands yet again.

"You're going to drain all our lakes!" Kayla shouts at me from my bed, irritated.

"Sorry." I walk back into my room and see her smiling at me. She's so beautiful. Her dark curls form around her naturally tanned skin and freckles.

I quickly turn back around and wash my hands one last time.

"Come on, Daniel. You're acting like we've never made out before."

"Coming. Sorry." I give her a sheepish grin and hop onto my bed next to her.

She leans over and starts kissing my neck as her fingers twist through my hair. I can't help but wonder when she last washed her hands. She moves over and sits in my lap, her lips never leaving mine.

One. Two. Three. Four. One. Two. Three. Four.

My heart speeds up. Fire races across my skin, leaving my fingers thick and dry. They feel scaly and dirty. I can't breathe, I have to shower now or my body is going to implode on itself.

"Kiss me, Daniel," Kayla whispers.

I ignore my oncoming panic and try to enjoy the moment as I kiss her soft lips and pull her closer.

Calm the hell down. Shit.

One. Two. Three. Four. One. Two. Three. Four. One. Two. Three. Four. One. Two. Three. Four. One. Two. Thr—

"I'm sorry. I can't." I push Kayla away from me and accidentally knock her to the floor before running to the bathroom shutting the door behind me.

"Dammit! What the hell are you doing, Daniel?" she yells at me from the floor.

I twist one of the shower knobs and get in, grabbing the closest bath brush and bar of soap.

"I'm coming in!"

"Wait—No!"

Kayla walks into the bathroom holding her middle. "What are you doing?" Her eyes widen. "Are you crazy? Daniel, stop! You're digging into your skin!"

I glance at her through the glass shower wall and turn my back towards her. "I need to get clean, then I can come back. Just let me get clean and I'll be better."

"No babe, you are very clean, you're going to scrub your skin off—Daniel, stop!"

I mumble, "I have to scrub every spot four times. Four times for eight seconds. I have to be clean for you. One. Two. Three. Four. One. Two. Three. Fo—"

"You're scaring me. I'm going to call your mom—"

"No! No, don't, I'm fine." What the hell am I doing? The water's freezing! I'm so stupid. "Um. Let me rinse off."

She hands me a towel as I step out of the shower. "Are you okay? I can still call your mom."

"Please don't. What are you going to tell her? Well, as I was making out with your son, he had a freak out moment and ran to the shower? After which I walked in and saw him naked?"

"Yeah, it doesn't look good... But you're scaring me, Daniel. You're spiraling out of control, and I don't know how to handle that."

"I know, I'm sorry."

Kayla gives me a quick hug, and all I can think is that I need to go get in the shower again because she was just on the floor.

She keeps talking, but her words are muffled by the sound of my heart pounding on the inside of my chest.

"I know your parents' divorce is hard on you, and it really sucks. Maybe you should talk to the school counselor or something? Or talk to me about it—talk to anybody about it."

She looks as if she could cry.

"I should go. Call me before you go to bed, okay?" She kisses me on the top of my head and grabs her bag.

The second she walks out the front door, I jump back in the shower.

## October 3

Kayla hasn't answered any of the texts I sent her last night. It kept me awake, knowing she's probably mad at me. I ended up cleaning the kitchen again and organizing the shelves in the living room. I wasn't sleeping anyway. I was surprised I didn't wake up Dad. He left the door to his office open and I could hear him snoring on the couch.

-Daniel

———

When did I start hating school? When did I stop hanging out with everyone and stop going to after school clubs? I can't even remember what clubs I signed up for this year. Little Readers. That was one of them, I'm supposed to be helping elementary kids learn to read after school. Shit, what if some little kid never learns to read because I ditched? And their whole life is ruined because of me?

I should check my email. What's my email password?

Why am I worrying about this now? I freeze in the middle of the carpeted walkway that separates the front doors to the rest of the school. Other students pour in around me like water from a broken dam, bumping and brushing past me as they go.

The rush of germs over my body consumes my senses like a flame. My skin itches under my clothes. It feels like beetles cutting, digging under my skin. This is all stupid. Stupid. Stupid. Stupid. Stupid. Stupid. Stupid. Stupid. I grab the right side of my head to help the circular words stop swirling around. Then instinctively grab the left side too, for balance.

One. Two. Three. Four. One. Two. Three. Four. One. Two. Three—

"Hey, Daniel! How are you? I've been worried." Kayla surprises me with a kiss and grabs a hold of my arm. She rubs her hand up and down my side, and it feels like glass shards sinking into my skin.

Worried? If she was so worried why didn't she answer any of my texts? I furrow my brows. I don't know how to answer her.

I need to wash my hands.

"Come on, I'll walk you to homeroom." She tries to take a step forward with her arm looped in mine, but I don't move. I can't move. Why won't I move? "Are you alive in there? We need to get to class, the bell rang." That's her annoyed voice.

"Uh, you go ahead, I'll catch up in a minute." I tap my fingers on my chest, counting to four with each tap. Why do I always feel so rushed when I'm at school?

"Let's just go—"

"PLEASE. I'll catch up. Up-up-up-up. Dammit."

"Um... sure... See you in a minute." She rolls her eyes. The glance she sends me over her shoulder is like a dagger to my heart.

Everyone is looking at me. They are all staring at me. What's my email password?

The bell rings again, but instead of sitting at my desk, my feet are glued to the floor.

Principal Johnson walks out of his office.

"Daniel? Why aren't you in class? Did you hear the bell ring?"

"Um. Yep. Yes. I did."

"So, what are you doing?"

"Don't have a clue." Because I can't remember my password,

and little Timmy is going to fail at life because I've been ditching Little Readers club and he's never going to learn how to read and it's all my fault. I shove my hands in my pockets, because that seems to be the only thing keeping my skin from melting off my fingers.

"Okay..."

"Uh, actually. I need to go. Right now." I turn and run out the door.

"Hey, Daniel? Daniel! I'm calling your parents." His voice is stern, annoyed. But that only makes me feel worse. Just another person I'm letting down.

I tap the door handle four times before jumping into the driver's seat of my car. I tear out of the school parking lot and quickly slow down so I don't cause an accident. It's a slow creep to my empty house where I race up the stairs, strip off all my clothes and jump in the shower.

One-two-three-four-one-two-three-four-four-four-four.... Dammit. One-two-three-four—

I squirt a bunch of soap on the scrub brush and run it over my skin, making sure I don't miss an inch. That should be enough scrubbing.

But I can't stop. I turn the water on as hot as I can stand it and do it again. Until all the faces of those I'm letting down wash out of my mind and down the drain.

I slowly turn the water off, making sure I catch every last drop on the top of my head, and grab a clean towel. The sound of my phone ringing floats into the bathroom, and the calm feeling dissipates. I rush over to my backpack and pull out my phone just as the call goes to voicemail.

"Shit." Seven missed calls from Mom. But I don't call her

back. I wait until the missed call number says eight, because eight feels more balanced and less stressful, and then call her back. "Hey—"

"Where are you?" Her voice is rushed and panicked. "Are you okay? Do you need me to come get you?"

I try to hold onto what little tendrils of calm I have left from my shower. "I'm fine. I just had to take a shower—"

"Daniel… You already had one this morning." Her sigh weighs heavy in my ear. And on my shoulders.

I don't say anything. What is there to say?

"I think maybe we should see a doctor again—"

"No! Don't say that. I said I'm fine. I'm headed back to school anyway." I look down at my hands, slightly raw from all the washing.

More silence. It might as well be fingernails on a chalkboard.

"What time will be you back at school?" she finally asks.

"Maybe before third period."

"Maybe?"

"Before third period."

"I'll call the school to let them know you're on your way."

"Okay." My heart sinks. I don't want to go back to school. But I have to go back to school or I'll lose my class standing.

"And Daniel?"

"Yeah?"

"I love you. You can talk to me, okay?"

"I know. I love you too, Mom."

## October 5

Garrett's coming over later. We stopped hanging as much this summer. I don't think it was completely on purpose. I focused on soccer and calling Kayla whenever she was awake while she was visiting family.

He and I have been best friends forever. I hate how awkward things are with him now. He's my only friend who knows about my OCD, but it's never bothered him—until recently. It's weird pretending everything's okay and he doesn't hate my girlfriend. He used to always complain about all the time I would spend with Kayla since we started dating... since we were sophomores.

I won't be able to handle him today if he acts all pissy. Just add him to the growing pile of people who are disappointed in me.

-Daniel

"Hey! What's up?" Garrett walks into my room and throws himself on my bed. The bed I just spent the last twenty or so minutes straightening up. "Dude, I forgot how clean your room always is."

"How's it going?" I take a seat on the bench under my window and suck down the urge to yell at him for wrecking my bed. Now I need to clean the comforter before tonight.

"You know, the usual. Surviving. Still dealing with my mom's douchebag boyfriend. The fucker." He rolls over and tosses a pillow at me. "What about you? I haven't really seen you since your last panic attack."

"Uh, yeah." I feel my face getting hot. "Can we forget about that? I've been under a lot of stress recently, and I don't want to talk about it."

"About your parent's divorce?"

"Yeah."

"Sure."

Awkward silence.

"So, other than that, what's going on?" Garrett asks.

"Nothing." I shrug.

A chasm widens between us, neither of us willing to take the first step.

More painfully awkward silence.

"Are you coming to Jace's Halloween party at the end of the month?" Garrett gets up and walks around my room, poking at random objects on my desk and bookshelves.

"I don't know. I didn't get an invite." Because everyone's been avoiding me. Not that I mind so much at this point.

"Yeah you did. He sent one to your school email, and I stuck a paper invite in your locker."

"Oh."

"'Oh' my ass." He sighs. "You forget your password again?"

I can't help but grin. It's both wonderful and terrifying when someone knows you this well.

"It's 'Larry-four-four-four-four-question mark.'"

"That's a stupid password."

"That was the point, so you wouldn't forget it." He picks up a small fuzzy soccer ball from my shelf and throws it at me.

My lame attempt to catch it sends his eyes rolling.

"Are you taking meds again?" Garrett flops back down on my bed.

"For what?"

"Fuck if I know. For your brain. Like when we were kids."

"For my OCD?"

He raises his eyebrows and stares at me. "Are we playing a game or are you going to tell me?"

I shake my head.

"Is that supposed to mean that you aren't back on meds, or are you refusing to tell me?"

"I don't need them. I'm not on them. I'm fine. Just a little stressed out. Now can you get off my bed?"

He rolls off of my bed onto the floor, grabs another soccer ball from under it and tosses it above his head. "Why not?"

"What, so you ignore me all summer, get all hot and cold at school with me, and then turn around and expect me to tell you all my deepest and darkest secrets?" My face grows hot as I straighten out my blanket and pillows on my bed again and place the fuzzy soccer ball back in its place. Only it doesn't feel right anymore. I squeeze it tight in my right hand, then squeeze it tight in my left hand, repeat, and place it back on its shelf again.

"Well, I'm going to go now... Come find me when you feel like holding an actual fucking conversation with me." Garrett jumps up and kicks the soccer ball across my room.

"Garrett, seriously?"

"Bye, man."

"Come on, don't be like that." It's too late. Instead of chasing after him, I get up to wash my hands as he runs down the stairs and slams the front door behind him on his way out.

"Asshole." I kick the soccer ball back under my bed and grab the smaller fuzzy ball again because it's not in the right place. Only this time I can't figure out why my shelf now feels so off-balance. "Ah!" I suck in a sharp breath and pull everything off the shelf so I can straighten it again.

With the shelf empty, the one right next to it feels off too, so I clear that one also. But I can't put everything away until I dust the shelf.

"Why…" I can't decide if I'm more annoyed at Garrett, or more pissed at myself for making an even bigger mess in my room. And forgetting my password again. I reach over for my phone on my nightstand and text Garrett, asking him for my password. He replies right away.

Garrett: Motherfucker. I knew it, you can't live without me.
Me: Password. Please.
Garrett: Larry4444?
Me: Thanks.
Garrett: Say it like you mean it.
Me: I'm sorry I'm an asshole.
Garrett: You are a fucking asshole. But I will allow it.
Me: :)

## October 15

I have a meeting today with the principal. I've been skipping too many classes. I knew what it was about before he told me. But I can't help it. I can't focus right now. There is too much going on in my life. I wish I could compartmentalize better.

-Daniel

—————

I drag my feet into the principal's office and freeze as I see both my parents sitting in chairs. Next to each other. My heart migrates to my throat.

"Come on in and have a seat, Daniel." Principal Johnson motions his hand towards the empty seat next to my dad.

"Hey." Dad pats my shoulder closest to him.

My hand automatically goes up to the other shoulder and squeezes it. "Hey."

Mom smiles.

"Let's go ahead and get started. I have a couple concerns I want to talk to you and your parents about." He pauses for a moment and gives me an awkward smile. As if that would make me feel any better about being here.

"As Daniel's parents, you are well aware that he was first in line to be the valedictorian of this year's graduating class. He has been one of our top-performing students since the day he set foot in my school three years ago. Not only that, but he is the captain of the soccer team and student body president, on top of being an active member in various clubs and organizations over the course of his high school career."

An active member in clubs... I think about little Timmy not learning how to read this year and a knot forms in my stomach. My name's on the roster, but I haven't stepped foot in any club this year yet. I haven't even been attending off-season soccer practice. But my parents don't know that. They don't know any of this. Another rock drops into the pit of my stomach. Well, they're about to find out. Fingers twitch as I try to find balance in my body under the copious amounts of stress.

"Yup, we're pretty proud of him." Dad smiles. "So what's the problem?"

"Daniel's grades are slipping, which has taken him out of the running to become the next valedictorian."

Yeah... I nod knowingly. Another rock drops, sinking me deeper. Shit. Hearing it out loud is more painful than I thought it would be. My lungs stop taking in oxygen for a moment as I avoid eye contact with everyone in the room.

"He has also dropped out of his role as student body president by simply not attending meetings. He's also been skipping his classes sporadically. His teachers, including myself, are beginning to worry about his well-being. I am afraid if things don't improve, he could be well on his way to losing some scholarships he has earned for college in the fall." He leans forward with his hands folded on his desk and continues to talk about me like I'm not here.

"We are concerned about this recent behavior, and I want to know how I—how *we* can help him succeed and finish his last year of high school on a strong note."

"Hmm." Dad looks at me. Is that disappointment? Concern? Maybe both.

One. Two. Three. Four. One—

Mom leans forward. "Daniel, talk to us. How can we help? Do I need to cut back working at the gallery? Because I will—"

"Mom, no."

"This is all our fault." She rubs her face. "William, we should have waited to tell him. We should have known this would happen—"

"Not here." Dad furrows his brows. "Daniel, this whole situation is difficult for all of us—more importantly, for you. But you can't keep letting your grades slide like this. School is still important."

"I know." Another few rocks drop into my stomach. "I just—I don't know. I'll try harder. I'm really sorry."

"Honey, you don't have to be sorry. Your Dad and I should have been paying better attention. We've both been so wrapped up with everything going on. I'm sorry."

"—We're sorry." Dad grabs my shoulders and squeezes them both, evenly.

"I'm going to make an appointment with our doctor." Mom pulls out her small calendar from her purse and writes a note.

"I don't need to see a doctor, Mom."

She nods, and mouths 'yes you do' before dropping her calendar back in her purse.

"I'm with her. I think it would be a good idea," Dad chimes in.

Principal Johnson nods in agreement, though seemingly confused. I haven't struggled with my OCD like this for years. I'm not even sure he knows what's going on.

"Daniel's dad and I are getting a divorce. There's a lot going on at home right now," Mom tells Principal Johnson.

"I see."

My heart pounds between my ears as beads of sweat glide

down my face. Why did she have to tell him that? Why did she have to tell him we're falling apart? That we're no longer going to be a team?

"Would you two mind if I talked to Daniel alone for a moment?" he asks.

Mom passes me a sympathetic glance and stands up.

"Sure." Dad clears his throat. "We'll wait for you outside."

My head floats on a string high above my body. I'm trying hard to bring it down, but I can't because the room is spinning at the same time and the thumping is too loud in my ears. I have to count. I have to count. One-two-three-four.

"Daniel." Principal Johnson walks around his desk and pulls a chair right in front of me and takes a seat. "If you ever need to talk, you can always come to me. We can even set up an appointment with the guidance counselor if you would like that better."

No, I don't want to talk to anybody about this. It's humiliating.

"Divorce is rough, son. I've been there with my parents. You can't hold it all in like this, you're putting way too much responsibility on your shoulders. You're still a kid, and you shouldn't be taking on this kind of pressure on your own. Skipping classes and dropping out on life isn't the way to go." He pauses and shakes my shoulder. "Hey, are you there?"

My hand automatically goes up to the opposite shoulder and shakes it before my hand falls back into my lap. I can't breathe and I feel as if I'm going to pass out. The sound of my breath is loud in my head.

He stands up and holds my arms over my head. "Breathe, Daniel. You'll be fine. Breathe." He lets one of my arms down and reaches into a nearby filing cabinet and pulls out a paper bag. "Here, breathe into this. I've had enough panic attacks in my office that I've started keeping a supply of these on hand."

I quickly grab the bag and breathe into it like it was my only source of oxygen. He sits back down in front of me.

"Do you want your parents to take you home?"

I shake my head.

"Would you like to finish out the school day?"

I nod.

"Are you going to skip any more classes?"

"No." Still breathing into the bag.

"I am sorry you have to go through this. It sucks doesn't it?"

Dammit. A few tears fall out of my eyes.

He puts a hand on my shoulder. "Hang in there, buddy."

I finally feel myself coming down from the ceiling. "Thank you. Can I go back to class now?"

"Sure." He reaches for the paper bag.

"Um, I think I may keep this with me."

"You're a good kid, Daniel. Don't let this be the defining moment of your life."

"Yeah."

"See you later."

## October 20

Garrett's been sending me texts non-stop, begging me to come to soccer practice today. Sometimes during the guys' off-season they'll practice with the girls' team. Not a lot of people show up. Unless you live, eat, and breathe soccer. Like Garrett does. Like I used to do.

Maybe I'll stop by, but I'm not going to join in. At least not this time. I don't feel like it. It'll be nice to see some of the other guys though.

-Daniel

The final school bell of the day rings as I slide into a seat behind a computer at the library to check my school email. I pull out my cell phone to get my password and place it on the table right next to the keyboard. Two hundred and four unread emails since school started. Shit. My heart jumps into my throat. Now I regret opening it.

I click on the first one that says URGENT and skim it. A warning about my seat as student body president being passed over to Shayla Jacobsen. Another email telling me that my class ranking has dropped. Also making Shayla the next in line to be valedictorian. Man, I bet she's never been so glad to be second in line to anyone before now. I check the class ranking status. Shit, I dropped forty-five places. My stomach sinks as I lightly tap the keyboard four times with each hand. It's only been one grading period, how the hell did this happen? I bite my bottom lip and pull in a deep breath through my nose to help intercept the incoming panic.

Little Readers club emails took up most of my email box for last month, but eventually stopped emailing. If they knew I wasn't responding, why didn't anyone come and talk to me in person? I'm not even on social media, and they know that. After four years of working with this club, they should know that. I hit select all and delete all the emails on that page. A moment of relief washes over me until the next page of unopened emails pops up. I empty my entire inbox, including the spam and trash folders. Much better. I squeeze my right hand into a fist, and then my left before stretching out my back. It feels like this has been the most productive part of my whole day so far.

My phone vibrates and I jump, it startles me. A few students look in my direction, and one glares and shakes their head at me. I roll my eyes and pick it up.

Garrett: Hey, you coming to practice?
Me: No—I didn't bring my cleats or a change of clothes.
Garrett: You can borrow my spares in my gym locker-code 25-
    6-12

My skin crawls at the thought.

Me: You have tiny girl feet.
Garrett: Wow, I'm hurt. Get your ass out here.
Me: I'll stop by, but I'm not practicing.
Garrett: Awesome!

I toss my phone into my bag and log out of the computer. He's not going to let it go if I don't stop by the field, so I might as well. I slowly make my way down the empty quiet halls, and out the back of the school, past the football field to the soccer and baseball fields across the street from the main back entrance of the school. It's a long trek from the school, but we have our own small gym and snack kiosk with public restrooms, so it's not that bad.

"Hey! Look who's here!" Jace yells out and runs towards me from the goal.

"Hi, Daniel."

"You coming to play?"

Several people shout from the center of the field where they're doing their warm-up stretches. Mostly familiar faces, some new. Freshmen maybe.

"Hey, man." Jace gives me a fist bump.

"Hey."

"Are you going to join us?"

"No, because he's a loser." Garrett jumps in and lightly shakes my right shoulder.

But before I can grab my left shoulder, he smacks my hand down and shakes that one too.

"I think it would be good for you if you joined us though," Garrett suggests.

"Maybe next time, yeah?" I shrug.

"Are you coming to my Halloween party?" Jace asks.

I look at Garrett for support, before responding, "I don't know, man. I'm not feeling up to being around tons of people right now…"

"It's not going to be a ton of people. Like twenty of us. We're going to watch some horror classics, eat pizza. You know, low key. Our home theater just got finished, and I'm excited to use it."

I look at Garrett again, but all he does is shrug.

I feel bad, I really do, because I want to go. But thinking about being around all those people makes me anxious. I know they're going to want to know how I'm doing. I know they're going to ask me a billion questions that I don't want to answer. I can't deal with that right now. "Maybe next time—"

"Whatever. I don't know why I wasted an invite on you anyway."

Garrett finally opens his mouth. "Hey, man. He's got a lot going on right now, don't push it."

"Yeah, we all do. It only looks different."

Garrett nods and shrugs before shoving his hands into the pockets of his sweats.

That hits me right in the stomach. "I'm not trying to act as if my problems are bigger than everyone else's. I just..." Maybe tell him about my OCD? Maybe that'll make him chill the hell out. I catch him glaring at me. Hell no-bad idea. "I'm not handling my parents' divorce very well."

"I get that, but why ditch all your friends? A lot of us have been where you are. You know?" Jace says.

My heart speeds up. Yeah, maybe others might understand but they won't understand everything. They don't understand how my whole world is crashing and burning around me. How there is so much more I can't control—that's controlling me.

"I gotta go, I'll talk to you later." I offer a limp wave and turn to leave the field.

"Yeah, whatever. No wonder your dad's leaving your ass,"

Jace spits out.

"Whoa, Jace, what the fuck?" Garrett sputters.

My mind empties. My body goes cold. My hands ball up into tight fists, and one goes flying into Jace's jaw.

"Oh, come on!" Garrett shouts as Jace yells and knocks me to the ground. With one of his hands pressing into my throat, his free fist pounds into my face twice before I throw my arms up, causing his blows to land on my forearms, over and over again.

I pull my right knee up as hard as I can and make contact with his groin. He lets out a wheeze and falls to the side. I push myself off the ground and let loose on his face. First my left, then my right hand until both are throbbing at the same speed.

"Daniel! Stop!" Garrett screams and pulls me off Jace. I spin and punch Garrett in the face.

"Get the hell off of me!" I snap and push Garrett away.

Jace gets off the ground and pulls my arms back as Garrett punches me in the chest.

"Enough!" Garrett screams. "What the hell is wrong with you?"

Jace lets go of my arms and I fall to my knees, clinging to my chest, trying to pull in a breath.

"Man, get the hell up," Garrett huffs.

Fuck this. I jump back up and tackle Garrett to the ground and let my fists fly. My bones pop with each blow slammed into Garrett. Sharp pain shoots into my wrists.

"Hey! Hey!!" Coach and another teacher run across the field towards us. I don't care, I keep swinging.

"Whoa! Knock it off!" The two men pull us apart. Garrett has blood coming out of his nose and a cut above his eye. It goes well with my soon to be two black eyes. Jace's face is just as swollen.

The coach yanks me to one side, and Garrett to the other, as the other teacher grabs Jace's elbow and pulls him farther away.

Shit, my hands. I have to wash my hands. This isn't all my blood. Their blood is on me. My heart slams into my rib cage as I struggle to pull in a breath.

"My office, now!" Coach pushes us towards the school, and the teacher and Jace follow.

The coach throws all three of us ice packs as we sit in silence in his office. Pressure builds around my eyelids as my vision slowly blurs. I can feel my eyes swelling shut.

"What the hell were you boys thinking? Beating on each other like a couple of punching bags! I should have you all suspended. You should be embarrassed. You boys are practically adults, and you are still picking fights with each other!" Coach lets out a loud sigh and rubs his face.

The other teacher leans against the filing cabinets behind the desk. He's standing there with a dumbfounded look on his face and his arms crossed.

"My soccer stars, friends, fighting like a bunch of little children." He plops down on his plush office chair. "What do you have to say for yourselves?"

"I'm sorry, it was my fault." I already know how much trouble Garrett is going to get in once his mom sees his face. Jace will have it a lot easier, mostly because he didn't throw the first punch. Punch. Hands. I hold my hands out slightly so I don't get any more of their blood on me.

Garrett clears his throat and looks at the floor.

"C-can I go wash m-my hands? Please?" I ball my hands into fists. I really need to wash my hands or I'm going to have a panic attack.

"Right now?" Coach asks.

"Yes."

"Go," he replies with a sigh.

"Thanks." I get up and try not to run down the hall.

I get to the bathroom and walk to the fourth sink, turn the hot knob off and on four times, put four pumps of soap in my hand and start scrubbing away at the blood and broken skin. I watch as the blood, their blood, washes down the drain. But what if it's too late? What if their blood as already made it into my bloodstream? Could one of them have some kind of bloodborne disease we didn't know about? And now I have it too?

One. Two. Three. Four. One. Two. Three. Four. One. Two. Three. Four. One. Two. Three. Four. One. Two. Three. Four.

Ten minutes go by and I am still scraping my hands with my nails under the warm water. I have to keep scrubbing. I have to make sure the blood's gone. My hands are disgusting. I have to wash them until they're clean. They're not clean. I need to take a shower. I need to get home. I make a mistake and look up, straight into the mirror. "Shit." My face looks like it got hit by a truck. I fill my raw hands up with water and splash it on my face. Except that only makes me feel worse as I feel the water entering every single scrape and abrasion on my skin.

I soap up and wash my hands again.

"Daniel? Daniel!" Coach peeks his head into the bathroom then runs over to me, yanking me away from the sink. "What are you doing?" He shuts the water off and pulls me back to his office. "Grab the first aid kit," he says to the other teacher.

I couldn't stop. I had to wash my hands. He doesn't understand.

Before I know it, they are putting Neosporin cream all over my hands and wrapping them in gauze.

"I'm going to call their parents and let them know what happened," the other teacher lets Coach know before walking toward the door.

"Wait, no, you don't have to do that—" Garrett speaks up and follows the teacher to the door.

"Have a seat, Garrett." Coach's stern voice causes him to sit back down immediately.

I sit there in silence, not sure what to say. But I can feel Jace's gawking gaze on me. He hasn't said a single word this whole time. Tears build up behind my eyelids, but my eyes are so swollen, it only deepens the pressure.

"One-two-three-four." I do the only thing that can keep me calm, I count under my breath and lightly tap my fingers on my chest. What the hell is wrong with me? I should have just walked away.

———

Mom pulls into the driveway and shuts off the engine. "Your dad will be home any minute. Dinner's already on the counter, go wait in the kitchen for us, please."

Her quiet tone makes me uneasy. "Mom—"

"I need a moment. Go eat."

I don't push it but quickly grab my bag and get out of the car. She didn't even acknowledge me or look at me when she picked me up from school. I've never seen her this mad before. I don't blame her, I'm mad at myself. But I hate her being so disappointed in me.

I drop my bag by the front door and drag my feet into the kitchen, placing my hands on the cold countertop as I take a seat. I'm not hungry. I just want to shower. Their blood could still be on me.

I don't give it a second thought as I run up the stairs and slam my bedroom door behind me, before stripping out of my clothes and tossing the bandages from my hands into the trash can by my desk. I turn the water up in my shower as hot as I can stand it before getting in. Thousands of needles stab into my face as the water trickles over my broken and bruised skin. I take in a breath through my teeth and force myself to stay put under the stream. It means it's getting clean. But that's not enough. I squirt a bottle of soap into a washcloth and rub it over my face, intensifying the stinging sensations. Then my hands. I rinse off and do it again, this time scrubbing the rest of my body. I'm not sure if I'm in the clear of any bloodborne diseases, but I rinse off one more time before shutting off the water and letting it drop off my body and run toward the drain.

"Hey, Daniel?" Dad knocks on my bedroom door.

I grab a towel and rush to grab my PJs. "Yeah?"

"Come on downstairs, we need to have a talk. Your mother told me what happened today."

I knew this was coming, but my stomach doesn't hurt any less. I straighten up my desk and tap four times on my sternum. It doesn't help me feel better. Shit. My face heats up even more as my blood pressure rises. At a snail's pace I make my way back downstairs.

"Have a seat." Dad points to the chair across from him in the living room.

Mom finally makes eye contact with me and shakes her head in disapproval. That hurts more than my black eyes and raw hands combined. I sit on the edge of the chair and lay my hands on my knees.

"Are you going to tell me what happened?" Dad asks.

"I thought Mom already told you?" My heart speeds up.

"I want to hear it from you."

I shrug, then shake my head. One, two, three, four. My fingers find their way to my sternum on their own.

Mom takes a seat in the chair beside me and takes my counting hand into hers and examines it. "Daniel..."

"I'm really sorr—it just happened. It was stupid, I know. I-I don't know, I really am sorry—"

"I know you are. I need to make an appointment with your doctor. I think you need to consider getting on something to help with your anxiety and—"

"No!" I pull my hand out of hers and stand up. "I'm fine. Jace and Garrett were just being—"

"Who cares what they were being, or saying or doing. You threw all your self-control out the window, Daniel. And I'm really worried that this divorce is affecting you way more than we anticipated. I'm the one that should be sorry." Mom wipes a tear from her cheek.

Did I do this to her? Make her cry? I hate myself.

"You're right, the divorce is crappy timing and we should be working through it…" Dad clears his throat, his voice wavering between calm and irate.

"Now is not the time to talk about that. Can't you see my son is struggling?" Mom snaps.

"*Our* son. And yes I can, it's because of the divorce."

"He needs to see a doctor, William—"

"He needs his parents to pay more attention to his needs!"

"I am paying attention! There is only so much we can do to help him with his anxiety and OCD. What's so wrong with him getting more help?"

"I never said there was anything wrong about that. Don't put words into my mouth." Dad crosses his arms across his chest and leans back into the couch.

Mom rubs her face and lets out a sigh.

I want to run upstairs to my room, but I can't. My feet are frozen to the carpet. Pressure builds in my face again as my blood pressure rises. My skin is on fire. I don't know how to make them stop. I don't know how to keep them together. I can't help but hate myself for not noticing them fall apart earlier. I could have prevented this from happening. I should have tried harder. This is my fault.

## October 21

I couldn't get my head to stop spinning this morning. My heart's been stuck in my throat ever since I woke up. I asked Mom if I could stay home today. She didn't say anything, but she nodded yes. She looked really sad, and that made me feel terrible. I know she's really disappointed in me. And that makes me feel like shit.

-Daniel

## November 12

What the hell is wrong with me? I can't keep doing this. My stomach hurts and I always feel like I'm going to throw up.

-Daniel

I drag my feet from the school library right into Spanish class before the bell rings. My class ranking has dropped again. I wonder how many people actually pay attention to their ranking? Or anyone else's? I tap my fingers on my thighs under my desk and will my heart to stop racing. But the more I try to control my breathing and racing thoughts, the faster my heart goes.

"Hey babe. We should catch up later, I feel like I haven't seen you in forever," Kayla whispers, kissing my cheek before taking her seat across the room. I brush my fingers on the opposite cheek so they would feel the same. But it doesn't help. Now I'm lopsided.

"Pull out your books and turn to chapter twelve. We're going to jump right into it today." Mr. Wilkersen leans against the front of his desk, textbook in hand.

Blood rushes through my ears, muffling sounds around me. My skin is thick and dirty. I need to shower. But class just started, so he wouldn't let me leave. Maybe I'll ask in twenty minutes if I can go to the restroom. Twenty-four minutes. Four minutes.

I dig the heel of my right palm into my right thigh, and do the same on my left side, hoping it'll help the thoughts slow down.

What are Mom and Dad going to say if they find out my ranking has dropped again? It's just going to cause them more stress and make them argue more. Any chance of them figuring things out are going to be lost because I can't keep my grades up. They're going to be so upset with me.

I should clean the kitchen when I get home. Maybe that'll help them relax. Maybe if they see I'm really trying to help them out they'll take more time to actually talk to each other instead of yelling at each other. When did they start yelling so much? We're supposed to be a team, and teams work shit out. No matter how bad it is.

I look up to see Mr. Wilkersen staring at me.

Oh shit. Please don't call on me. Please don't call on me... I avert my eyes. I should have asked to go to the restroom sooner.

"Daniel? Can you answer the question please? En español por favor."

I dig one finger at a time into my leg. One, two, three, four.

"Did you hear me?" Mr. Wilkerson says, his voice louder this time.

"Uh, I-uh." My stomach turns. Everyone's looking at me. Sweaty palms. My palms are sweaty. The room spins. "W-what was the question?"

"Are you alright? Do you need to go to the nurse? You're looking a little pale." He walks over to me and tries to put his hand on my shoulder.

I push his hand away. Doesn't he know I'm disgusting? Why would he do that?

"Hey." He leans in. "Are you okay?"

"Stop talking to me!" Dammit, that was too loud. "I'm sorry. C-can I go please?"

"Of course. Go to the nurse."

I nod and try to stand up, but I can't. My legs feel as if they have been cemented to the floor. The lights are flickering too much, my breathing is too loud, everyone is staring at me now. Why are they all staring? They probably know how gross I am. Why didn't I leave earlier? I try to pull in a deep breath, but it gets stuck in my throat. Now I can't breathe. My chest hurts.

One, two, three, four. One, two, three, four. Out of nowhere, flood gates open and tears drench my shirt. But now I'm too nervous to move. My whole body's paralyzed.

"Daniel, can you hear me? Let's get you to the nurse, okay?" Mr. Wilkerson attempts to help me get up.

"N-no, don't touch me!" I grab my stomach and double over, hoping that will make the world around me stop spinning.

"Class dismissed to the library. Go. Now." The room quickly empties, leaving only Mr. Wilkerson and Kayla alone to stare at me.

"He's having a panic attack," Kayla tells Mr. Wilkerson.

"You're probably right." He kneels on the floor beside my desk.

"Don't touch me-don't touch me-don't touch me-don't touch me."

Mr. Wilkerson tells Kayla to go get the nurse, and she quickly leaves the room "Daniel, can you hear me? I need you to focus."

"One, two, three, four. One, two, three, four. One, two, three, four. One, two, three, four. One, two, three, four." I beat on my chest with my fist, trying to get myself to calm down. But I can't. Mr. Wilkerson is talking to me, I see his lips moving, but I can't hear a sound above the blood rushing through my ears.

Kayla rushes back in the room with the school nurse, who promptly grabs my arms and puts them over my head.

"Kayla, can you get him a glass of water, please? Breathe in through your nose and out through your mouth."

No, no, no, no. She's touching me. I need to shower. I need to shower—"Don't touch me!" I yank my arms out of her grasp and try to push away from her, causing me to fall and knock the desk over.

Kayla flinches and drops the paper cup full of water.

I watch it fall to the floor in slow motion.

Mr. Wilkerson and the nurse try to help me stand up.

"Stop touching me! Dammit! Everyone stop fucking touching me!" I scramble out of the fallen desk and start rocking on the floor while pounding my fist into my chest. "One-two-three-four-one-two-three-four-one-two-three-four-"

"I'm calling EMS. Try to keep anything away from him that he could hurt himself on." The school nurse leaves the room. The bell rings and a crowd of students quickly assembles by the door.

"One-two-three-four-one-two-three-four." They're looking at me. They are all looking at me. Shit. Shit. Shit. Shit. My shirt clings to my skin from sweat. The stench fills my nostrils and I want to gag. Get it off! Get it off! The shirt can't come off fast enough. It feels as if it weighs a ton as I try to throw my soaked T-shirt across the room.

"Kayla, go tell my students to go to the library and close the door please." Mr. Wilkerson tries getting closer to me. "Daniel, how can I help you?"

"Don't touch me, don't touch me. One-two-three-four-one-two-three-four." Heart racing, ears buzzing, stomach leaping, head pounding, arms twitching. One-two-three-four-one-two-three-four. I'm dying. My breath grows louder in my ears as the corners of my vision slowly darken.

The nurse walks back into the room with two paramedics and a gurney.

"Daniel, these men are here to help you." She turns to the paramedic. "He won't let anyone near him."

The men approach me. "It's Daniel, right? My name's Daniel, too, but you can call me Dan. Only my mother calls me Daniel, and it usually means I'm in trouble." He holds out his hand like I should shake it, then lets it down.

"Listen, Daniel, it seems like you're having a really bad day. Looks like you're having trouble breathing. You've taken your shirt off and you don't want anyone to touch you. We'd like to help you get through this, but we're gonna have to work as a team. We've called your parents and they're pretty worried about you. We'd like to take you to them, but we need your help. Can you get on the gurney for us?"

I try to push myself farther into the wall, but instead I slip and slam my left shoulder into the floor. A sharp pain races down my arm. I groan and cradle my left side, but my right side is calling out. It doesn't feel even. I shake my head. I just want to go home. My right side screams louder, begging to feel the balance. Wanting everything to be made right again.

Slowly, I press my right shoulder into the wall behind me, but it's not enough, and it's a different kind of pressure. That's not right. Shit, that only makes me feel worse. This time I turn more towards the wall and bang my right shoulder into it. I do it again, only harder. And harder again, and harder—

"Whoa there." Dan places his hand on my arm.

"Get away from me!" I scream. Or was that me? My brain doesn't recognize the high-pitched voice ripping out of my throat. I hit my right side too hard on the wall this time and hit my left side to match that same feeling. Everything feels off, I need to fix it, I have to fix it. Why can't I fix it?

Dan looks over to the other paramedic and Mr. Wilkerson. His words sound like the wind. Their voices keep fading in and out, I can't catch everything they are saying.

Mr. Wilkerson nods, and before I know it, the three men and the nurse grab my arms and legs. They fight to get me on the gurney.

"Don't touch me! Put me down! Please let me go! Kayla! Kayla-don't let them take me! Don't touch me!" I flail my limbs to get free, but they are too strong. They're going to take me and lock me up. No, no, no, no. One-two-three-four-one-two-three-four-one-two-three-four-one-two-three-four.

"Get his legs strapped down," the paramedic directs.

Tears stream down my face. My right side screams out again, begging for everything to be put in balance, screaming for everything and everyone to be put back in their place again. "Please..." The cold straps dig into my sweaty skin. I have to wash them off. I have to wash everything off.

Dan places an oxygen mask over my face as they quickly roll me out of the room and down the hall. I can't fight them anymore. My body is too heavy. It sinks further and further into nothingness as we roll down the hall, passing dozens of other students staring at me through the doorways of the passing classrooms.

One. Two. Three. Four.

———

"Is he going to be all right? How long does he have to stay here for?" The muffled sound of Mom's voice breaks through the darkness as it slowly dissipates around me.

I attempt to pull myself up, but my slow drunken movements are being held down by a thick strap that is across my chest. I try to kick my legs, but they too are tethered to the bed.

Hospital. I'm in the hospital. The suffocating oxygen mask digs into my face.

"Whoa, lay still, you're okay. You're safe." Dad reaches over and brushes my hair out of my eyes.

I move my lips, but nothing comes out. My stomach hurts. My head hurts. Everything hurts.

A doctor walks over to me and shines a light in my eyes. "Hello, Daniel. My name is Dr. West. How are you feeling?" She pushes her black braids behind her ear as she jots down some notes.

I open my mouth to let out a moan.

"You had a hard day today. I gave you a little something to help you relax." She motions over to a random nurse in the room. "Take these straps off of him, would you?"

The nurse walks over to remove the straps. The cats on her scrubs make me dizzy.

"Don't try to sit up. I don't want an accident in case you still feel woozy." Dr. West checks my vitals.

With jerky movements, I knock the mask off my face.

"What…"

"What happened?" She continues checking me out without looking up.

"Uh… huh." I wince as I try to sit up. Both of my shoulders feel bruised.

"You had a panic attack. Have you been having those a lot recently?"

I look over at my parents standing at the foot of the bed. Their faces covered with complete fear and worry. I look back at the doctor. Her voice is soothing and helps me feel calm.

"When was the last time you had a panic attack? Can you remember right now?"

"A lot."

"Have you had one like this before?"

I shake my head no. Then shrug. Then nod. When I was little. She places the oxygen mask back on my face.

"I would like to keep you for a few days or so for observation."

"It's okay, honey," Mom whispers as she wipes her face dry.

Dad nods and squeezes Mom's shoulder. I'm shocked to see them so close to each other.

"We will have you moved up to the fourth floor, west wing in a few hours. For now, get some rest." Dr. West turns to leave.

"What's on the fourth floor?" I ask.

"Oh, it's where we can keep a better eye on you to make sure you're doing all right."

"What?" Panic beats its way through the center of my chest again.

"It's nothing to be afraid of. It is a safe place to keep you while under observation. Your parents and visitors can still come and see you."

"It's going to be okay, Daniel." Mom forces a weak smile.

"Of course it will!" Dr. West smiles one last time as she walks out of the room.

One... two... three... four...

## November 15

I've been in the hospital for three days. What the hell is wrong with me?

-Daniel

———

"Hey." Kayla knocks on the door of my hospital room but doesn't come in.

I close the journal Mom brought me and slide it under my pillow. My cheeks heat up and a smile plasters itself on my face. But only for a moment.

She slowly makes her way to my bed and whispers, "You're in a psych ward. I had to go through a security check before they let me in." Then holds up a book. "It suddenly doesn't feel appropriate to bring you this book. It's for English class, but it's still a good book."

"You don't have to whisper," I whisper back before speaking up. "It is kind of weird being in here. I'm trying not to think about it too much. Plus, don't feel bad. *Catcher in the Rye* is a horrible read anyway." I try to smile again.

She shrugs. "I liked it."

"Thanks, Kayla." I sit up as she awkwardly wraps her arms around me and gives me a hug. "I'm not going to break."

"I was so scared. You were... It was just really upsetting."

"The only thing I can remember is the feeling that I was dying. But maybe that's a good thing I can't remember all the details."

A tear forms in her eye.

"No-no-no, don't do that, everything's okay now." My heart slams into my chest. I hate seeing her cry. Especially when there is nothing I can do to fix it. Yet.

She nods. "What happened? Why were you like that? You kept trying to hurt yourself."

"I, uh—" Regret drops a few stones into my stomach. All of these years, I could have told her. Even when I started having problems again, I should have told her. I was too afraid of what she would think. I'm still too afraid of what she will think. I tell her anyway. "I have... it's my OCD. There's just been a lot going on and anxiety's really been messing with my head. Usually I can control it—the OCD—but... I don't know. It got away from me this time, I guess."

She laughs. "Seriously? OCD? Honestly, what happened?"

I shrug and stare at my hands. That's not the reaction I was expecting.

"Sorry. I know you're a neat freak and germaphobe, but... OCD?" she repeats.

"Ha. Yeah..."

"How long have you had it? Is it going to go away again?" She takes a step back and sits on the arm of a nearby chair.

I shake my head. She's disappointed. My stomach turns, I've been doing that to everyone recently—disappointing them. "I was diagnosed when I was a kid. Maybe kindergarten, or first grade."

"Wow."

"Yeah."

"How come you never told me?" Her voice is soft, but I can't read the expression on her face.

"I just..." I shrug. "It hasn't been something that's affected my day-to-day life until recently, you know? I mean it did in some ways, but it was manageable. I didn't think it was that big of a deal. There never seemed to be an appropriate time to drop an, 'oh, by the way, I'm OCD and struggle with severe anxiety sometimes.' I'm sorry. Maybe I should have told you a long time ago, but I'm telling you now. Please don't be mad at me."

"I'm just glad you're okay."

"Thanks. Me too." Silence envelopes us for several moments. I can't look at her right now. She probably hates me.

Out of nowhere she bursts out crying. "Daniel, it was horrible! You were freaking out and yelling—you wouldn't let anyone touch you. They had to manhandle you onto the gurney. I was so scared!"

There it is. I reach for her and she sits on the bed with me.

"I'm sorry, I told myself I wasn't going to cry." She wipes her tears on her sleeve.

One. Two. Three. Four. One. Two—

"How long do you have to stay here? You look a lot better, does that mean you can go home soon? And come back to school?"

—Three. Four. One. Two. Three. Four. One—

"Daniel?" She wipes her face again and grabs a hold of my hand.

Her hands are wet, and she's touching my hand. Why-why-why-why is this bothering me now? I've seen her cry dozens of times and wiped her tears with my own hands. I hold my breath to try and make my heart slow down as it jumps on the merry-go-round of thoughts.

I need to wash my hands.

I can't imagine what she thinks of me now. She probably

hates me. I would hate me. I'm an awful boyfriend.

I need to wash my hands.

What if this is it for her and she's just being nice? What if I never actually leave this place and they keep me and I miss the rest of my senior year? Why is she still crying?

I need to wash my hands.

Why did she wipe her face then grab my hand? She should have washed her hands. I need her to stop holding my hand. Why am I thinking about her? She did nothing wrong. What the hell is wrong with me?

I need to wash my hands now!

One. Two. Three. Four. One. Two. Three. Four.

Kayla reaches for my other hand. "Daniel? Are you okay?"

"I can't, I'm sorry—" I push her away and run to the sink in my room where I frantically start scrubbing my fingers in warm water. One. Two. Three. Four.

I have to wash my hands.

Kayla pushes the nurse call button and runs over toward me. "Hey, I didn't mean to—I don't know what to do—Daniel, look at me, please!"

"I'm sorry. I'm sorry but I need to wash my hands—"

Two nurses walk into the room. "What's going on?"

"He just freaked out and now he won't stop washing his hands—I don't know what to do."

"It's okay, I'll help him. Come on, Daniel, let's get away from the sink, you should lay down and rest." One of the nurses turns the water off and the other male nurse places a hand on my right shoulder.

My heart jumps on a racetrack. I reach up to my left shoulder and squeeze it before knocking his hand off me. I don't want them to touch me. I don't want anybody to touch me. "Stop it. I have to start over now—I'll be fine, just let me finish."

"Do you have control? Or does washing your hands have control over you?"

The sensation of a million ants covers my body.

He keeps talking to me. "Daniel, look at me. Can you look at my eyes? Good, try to calm down. Breathe in and out. Good, good. Can I count with you? Let's count together. One, two, three, four. Good. One, two, three, four."

He counts with me to four, eight times in a row. I am more focused, but the urge to wash my hands is still there. I know it makes no sense. I finally let him lead me to the bed as the other nurse straightens up my blanket for me.

"I am now going to give you something that should help you focus, all right?"

I nod. My stomach hurts. I want to throw up, then throw myself off a cliff. The other nurse hands me a tiny paper cup with two white pills in it and a cup of water. I take it without hesitation. Anything to make my heart and stomach cooperate again.

"You got a little stuck. Didn't you?"

I nod again and look around, trying to spot Kayla.

"Oh, your friend left. Sorry about that."

Goosebumps cover my skin. Why did she just leave me like that? A vice squeezes my heart. She can't leave me like that. Can she?

"It got a little intense for her. But that's okay. Being in a hospital is a lot for some people to handle."

Of course it is. Especially when I'm locked in a psych ward. Captain of the soccer team. Former student body president.

Former predicted valedictorian. Now I'll forever be known as the crazy kid who lost his shit during Spanish class because he couldn't handle his parents getting a divorce.

"Your parents will be here soon. How about you try and get some rest before they and the therapist show up?"

"Sure." I can't argue with him, the pills are now filtering through my veins, helping me relax and calm down.

Very relaxed...

## November 16

Everything's worse. It's stupid. It doesn't even make sense to me. I know these coping habits are just a side effect from all the stress, but I'm afraid that they won't go away. What if I keep getting worse? That scares me.

Kayla has not been back to see me. I don't have my phone so I can't text her either. What a mess. On top of everything else, the doctor made a comment about keeping me here a little longer. I don't want to stay here. I'm fine. Just stressed. But any normal human would be stressed if they kept on disappointing everyone in their life.

Maybe I was in an accident or got really sick or something, and I've actually been in a coma this whole time... And none of this is real. I'll wake up soon and everything will be back to normal and I can move on with my life.

If only...

-Daniel

## November 17

They're keeping me here another week. I overheard the doctor talking to my parents earlier. She told them that they were not going to move me to the children's psych hospital, that I'm doing just fine here. As long as they have space for me here in the psych wing at the general hospital, I can stay… That scared the shit out of me. I'm meeting with the hospital therapist again today, Dr. Hannah. He seems nice enough. Weird. But nice.

-Daniel

"Hey, Daniel. How are you doing today?" Dr. Hannah grabs the folder hanging by my door.

"I'm fine."

"Great! Follow me, please." He grins and I follow him down the hall to an empty room with a couch, an overstuffed chair, and a metal chair in the far corner. "Pick your seat."

I take the metal chair in the far corner.

"By all means, take the comfy chair."

I glance at the soft brown chair with an overstretched couch cover clinging to its last thread. "I'm okay." It probably doesn't get cleaned that often.

"Okay." He takes a seat on the couch, closest to me.

My stomach hurts again. One, two, three, four.

"That's good. The good ol' chest tap. Is this something that you do often?"

"Oh." I didn't realize I was doing that. "No. I mean yes. Well… sometimes."

"Hmm. Does it help you focus?"

"It happens when I'm nervous or having a hard time focusing sometimes, I guess."

"I see." Dr. Hannah writes down something on the clipboard. "How are you feeling on the new medication?"

"Fine. A little sleepy. I don't feel as stressed out."

"Good, good."

"Hey, when do you think I can go home?"

"That's a very good question. Well, as soon as we feel like the medication is helping. We don't want to send you home, only to have you come right back here again. But, if you need to come back, that is perfectly okay too. We are always ready to help."

"Right."

"Soon though. Just focus on getting better, don't worry about the time. We want to make sure you have a good support system set up when you leave, with a good therapist, and to make sure your teachers are on board with the plan."

"The plan? My teachers?" Why does everyone have to know?

"Your parents mentioned you are falling behind and struggling in school. We want to make sure you have all the help you need. All completely normal."

Normal. I now hate that word. I wish I had words to explain how much I hate that word. My stomach falls to the floor. "Ha. You're kidding?" There goes my whole senior year.

"What is there to kid about?"

"I mean, I know I'm a little OCD, I was diagnosed as a kid. I was on meds for a little while, and it pretty much went away. This isn't a big deal or something new. I'm fine."

"Hmm. There's no such thing as a little OCD. You either are, or you're not. Unless you just have OCD tendencies, then I guess you could say you're 'a little' OCD. There are just different levels of severity." He looks through my chart. "You are full-blown OCD in all its glory. That's not a bad thing though. It just means you have a few more challenges than the average joe."

I roll my eyes. "I'm fine, I just need something for my panic attacks. I can get my OCD under control again. I'll be *fine.*" The more my chest tightens, the more my cheeks heat up.

"There's that word again: *fine.*" He smirks. "'You keep on using that word. I do not think it means what you think it means,'" he says in a cheap Spanish accent before returning to his normal voice. "It's good to be a little skeptical until you understand all the reasons for us wanting to be a bit more cautious. Tell me this, Daniel, how many showers did you have this morning?"

I don't want to answer that. No one stopped me. Plus I'm in a hospital, everyone should be showering more often. Thinking about it makes me want to wash my hands again. I squeeze my hands into fists and cross my arms.

"How many times did you get up to wash your hands when you were done with your showers, before I came and saw you?"

"Well I—"

"I'm not saying this to get you upset, I genuinely want you to think about what you are doing and be aware that you have options to help you."

"But I—"

"If you can tell me that you do not, right now in this moment, have the urge to get up and wash your hands, then I will get up and leave. I will even sign the papers and have you released."

My stomach falls through the floor and lands in the parking garage, five stories below. One. Two. Three. Four. One. Two. Three. Four. One. Tw—

"It's perfectly fine to need help. Heck, even I see a therapist, and I am one! I think everyone should see a therapist, whether they think they need it or not. Um, you're tapping your fingers on your chest again."

"Oh." I slide my hands under my thighs. "Sorry."

"No need to apologize. You're not hurting me. I just want you to be more aware of your actions."

"Yeah, sorry—I mean. Of course." Heat rises up in my cheeks.

Mom walks past the room and pretends not to look in the window. Dad peeks his head back and waves, points to a brown paper sack, and sinks back away from the window.

Dr. Hannah chuckles. "Well, that's it for now Daniel, I will see you tomorrow at the same time. If you need to talk sooner, just have me paged." He walks over to the door and opens it. "It's good to see you Mr. and Mrs. Quincy. The room's all yours!"

"Thank you. Hey buddy, brought you that burger." Dad walks in with Mom and nearly sets the bag down on the arm of the overstuffed chair.

"Uh-lets go to my room." I stop him. "I need to clean up."

Mom kisses my shoulder. "Well hello to you too."

I stumble and accidentally knock my shoulder into the door frame on the way out and freeze in the hall. Mom and Dad step aside and let me knock my opposite shoulder. It still doesn't feel right. I lean back towards the door frame again.

"That's enough, I think you need to give your shoulders a break," Dad says and gently guides me back to my room.

"I agree. Let's get your mind onto something else. Like that burger," Mom chimes in.

It's nice having them together, and not arguing with each other. I like seeing them smile. Even if they're not looking at each other.

## November 19

Another day full of happy pills and hospital gowns. Another day of rushing to the sink to wash my hands, hoping no one will see me. Another day with no visits from Kayla. Or Garrett. Or anyone else. Except my parents.

Maybe everyone is afraid of me now.

I hate the anxious feelings I keep having. It's been weird being here for so long and not doing any of my morning rituals. It makes everything feel unbalanced in a way. I've had these silly rituals and habits since I was younger, and I've known they don't all make sense, but I have to do them. My parents thought it was because I was a very particular child. All books and pens had to be straight and level, and in alphabetical order. My room always had to be cleaned, my shelves had to be symmetrical. If I played outside for a while, I was always more than happy to take a shower. Never baths. Baths are gross.

None of this bothered Mom or Dad growing up until I started flinging my body into walls in fourth grade when I would feel unbalanced. I came home from school one day covered in bruises. A kid accidentally knocked me over on the playground and I landed on my left side really hard. It was sore and throbbing, but my right side felt like nothing. So I flung myself on the ground over and over again on my right side until it felt the same as my left side.

Mom cried for a month. Dad had to take me to therapy for the first several months because Mom felt guilty that my OCD was getting worse. She thought she could have prevented it. That it was all her fault.

It's not her fault.

-Daniel

## November 20

Another day with no visitors.

Now that I've lost my shit, flipped my lid, dropped all my marbles (again), no one has come to see me. I wonder if I scared Kayla so much that she went and warned everyone off. Or maybe they are really keeping me here forever, or are preparing to send me to the damn psych hospital on the other side of town.

I wouldn't blame them. Before I sat down to write, I washed my hands four times in a row. It's killing me to fight this feeling to go wash them again. Why do I need to wash them again when I haven't touched anything but my notebook and pen? Maybe there is a lobotomy sometime in my future...

It scares me being like this. Especially when it wasn't such a big deal before.

-Daniel

———

"Why, good day to you sir!" Dr. Hannah walks into my room with a stupidly huge smile on his face. "We're going to hang out in your room today. Our usual place is *ocupado*."

"Ha. Hey." I wish my mom had stayed for this.

"How are you feeling?"

"Fine. A little tired. Less anxious. But it's still there."

"Good, good. Well, it may always be there, our goal is to help you learn how to manage it so you can go about your day like any other individual on the planet."

"Good." I look at my hands, I can't help it. I get up and walk over to the sink and start washing them. Four pumps of soap. Scrub for forty long seconds. Rinse for four long seconds. Four more pumps of soap. Scrub for forty seconds. Rinse for four long seconds. Four pumps of soap—

"Take your time. But make sure you're in control. If you don't feel like you're in control, tell me and I will help you."

I stop to splash water over my face. One, two, three, four. "Yeah, sorry." Stop it, Daniel. Stop, stop, stop, stop. Dammit.

"No, no need to apologize." He takes a seat on the rolling chair. "When do you think all this compulsiveness started?"

I continue to wash my hands at the sink. "I don't know. Three, four… maybe I was five? I was in therapy for a while and on medication for a few years. I figured out a routine and how to keep myself under control. Well, I *was* in control—until my parents told me they were getting a divorce."

"That must be hard, thinking your parents would always be together."

"They haven't always been together. He's actually my stepdad, they got married when I was in the third grade." Why did I even say that? Why did that have to pop into my head right now? I haven't thought about that for years. He is my dad. I've never called him my stepdad in my whole life. The hummingbird takes flight between my ears.

"Really? Where's your biological dad?"

"I don't know."

"Oh?"

"Yeah, no idea where or who he is."

"Have you been curious about who he is? Do you ever want to search for him?"

"No, why would I? He obviously didn't want me, so why

waste my time?"

I turn the water off. Then I turn it back on. No, I don't need to wash my hands again. I turn it back off and freeze, staring at the sink, fighting the urge to fill my palms with antibacterial soap again.

"Come have a seat." Dr. Hannah stands up and tries to guide me back to the bed without touching me. I give in and sit down, still staring at the sink.

The sheets are itchy. When was the last time they were cleaned? Now I need a shower, he needs to go so I can shower.

The sink is dripping, I didn't turn the knobs tight enough. I need to go wash my hands again. No. No. No. NO. Stop it, what the hell am I doing?

One-two-three-four-one-two-three-four-one-two-three-four-one-

"Focus buddy, look at my eyes, what's going through your head right now?" He waves a hand in front of my face.

"What? Oh. Um, nothing, nothing, I'm fine. Fine. Fine. Fine." Dammit.

"Yes you are." I get up to wash my hands again. Dr. Hannah doesn't say a word, instead he starts writing in the folder he brought with him and watches me.

Why is he watching me? Why is he staring at me? He thinks I'm a freak. He thinks I'm broken. This will only stop when I'm dead. It might be better to be dead. Maybe I should kill myself. A wave of nausea consumes me, followed my prickly goosebumps. Why would I think that? "Uh, I can't stop. I can't stop—" I squeeze my eyes shut and hit the wall with the side of my fist.

"All right, you're all right. You have to practice a level of self-control that most humans will never have to reach in their lifetime. You can do this. I am going to go ahead and get something to help you relax." He steps out of the room for a moment to talk to a nurse.

"One-two-three-four."

## November 26

Today was a better day. I didn't get stuck on many loops, and when I did, I could stop them. The medication has been helping my anxiety a lot. I feel like most of the time if I can get the anxious feelings to calm down, I would be able to control myself better.

But now I'm really nervous for other reasons. I never told anyone about my dad not being my bio dad. Not even Garrett. I thought if I believed it hard enough, and tried to forget what happened before he came along, everything would be fine. If I tried hard enough he would stay. And he did, which meant everything I was doing was working. But now it's not, and I still don't know how to fix it.

Mom brought a huge pile of homework for me to work on. I thought it would have stressed me out, but the distractions have been nice. Dad went to my school and gathered all my books from my locker too.

They've been really nice to each other lately though. At least around me. It's soothing to see them act like they like each other again. I like that.

-Daniel

## November 28

They are letting me go home today. With a list of medications, and a scheduled follow-up visit with my doctor… and I have to see a shrink a couple times a week. Great.

-Daniel

## December 3

Today I go back to school. I caught up with most of my homework over Thanksgiving when I was in the hospital. I have to stop by the guidance counselor's office first before school starts.

School. The place where I had a mental break down. Where everyone stares at me and whispers behind my back. The place where all my friends disappeared without giving me a second thought.

Should be fun.

-Daniel

———

I wait in my car until the last warning bell for the first period rings. Empty halls mean no people. No people means no weird stares or glances. I tap the steering wheel four times and squeeze it tight with both hands before getting out.

Ready.

Not ready. But do I have a choice?

Taking my time, I weave my way through the senior parking lot to the main entrance. I suck in a deep breath and drag my feet past the flagpole to the front doors, using my elbow to push the door open.

"Daniel! I heard you were coming back today. It's nice to see you." Principal Johnson offers a high five. "How are you doing?"

I hesitate, and offer a fist bump instead. "I'm okay. Sorry I'm late."

"Don't even worry about it. I'm just glad you're here."

"Thanks." It feels strange to be back. I feel like I've been gone at least a decade.

"Do you have any place you have to be right now?" He steps right back into principal mode.

"Mrs. Lewis' office."

"I'll let you go—but please, if you need anything, or need to talk, you know where my office is." His smile is sympathetic. Almost sad.

It makes my stomach turn. I know he's just doing his job, but I'm not used to this side of him. I nod and follow the blue line on the floor towards the counselor's office. I really hope the whole day isn't like this. Less attention is better.

The moment I step through the door, Mrs. Lewis' eyes light up. "Hi, Daniel! It's so good to see you. I'm glad you're back." I follow her into her office and she motions to a chair in front of her desk for me to sit.

"Yeah, I'm surprised I made it myself."

"Why's that?"

I shrug.

"I wanted to check in with you before you dive back into school and to see how you're doing. You can stop by to see me anytime you need to, even if it's during one of your classes. We want to make sure that you know you are supported. And that we are fully aware of your OCD. I don't want you to worry or feel stressed about it. How are you doing this morning?"

"Does everyone know about that?"

"Well, just the important people. The principal, your teachers, other staff members. Your parents filled us in on what we need to know. We want to help you finish your senior year strong by any means possible."

"Right." The hummingbird between my ears warms up.

"Have you caught up on your homework, or do you think you need more time?"

"Most of it. I still have some things in Calculus and Spanish I need to finish." The bell rings.

"That's okay. Take your time. Try to have it turned in before Christmas break. You won't get any late marks."

I nod.

"Well, thanks for stopping by. You should get to class. I mean it though, anytime you need to talk, I am always here."

"Yeah, thanks." I make my way to my next class. All my books are still in my backpack, so I don't need to stop by my locker. I hold my breath and try to avoid getting touched, but I don't have to try that hard. The other kids are doing a good enough job staying away from me. As if OCD and anxiety are contagious.

I drag my feet into the class and sit in my regular seat, right next to Kayla. She glances at me quickly and looks back down at her desk, almost as if she is pretending I am not there.

My heart jumps into my throat. I don't know how to react, so I ignore her, too.

"Daniel!" Garrett bursts into the room and steals the desk in front of me before anyone can sit down in it. "How are you, man? I haven't seen you in fucking forever. Are you feeling better? Do they have you on lots of drugs? I bet they gave you the good kind. Are you high? Do you feel high?" He's all smiles.

"Uh, yeah, I mean no, I'm fine. I don't feel high. Not really." He hasn't spoken to me in weeks, he didn't even come to see me in the hospital. No texts, nothing. I glance around the classroom. All eyes are on me. They are all looking at me,

Daniel the freak who tried getting naked in the Spanish classroom.

"Man, sorry I never came to see you. You know how busy it gets and shit. And... *hospitals*." He shivers.

"Yeah, don't worry about it. I get it."

"It's so good to have you back!" He grabs my shoulder and gives it a squeeze. Then squeezes my other shoulder before I could get to it. "What are you doing after school today? A bunch of us are going to the bowling alley to hang out. Just us guys. I figured you would need it after Kayla dumped you. You're a free agent!"

Wait. "What?" I look over to Kayla who blushes and slouches more into her chair. "Yeah. I guess I am." I'm an idiot. I should have known after she started ignoring me.

The hummingbird takes flight leaving nothing but my heart pounding into my rib cage. Come on, class is just starting, don't do this now. One, two, three, four—

The bell rings again. Relief.

"All right class, have a seat so I can take roll." The teacher in the front of the room begins calling out names as I look over towards Kayla, who is now whispering to the girl behind her and awkwardly peeking in my direction.

My stomach sinks as I slouch into my chair, wishing it would swallow me whole. She was my first and only girlfriend. I thought she was better than this. I thought we were better than this.

## December 10

I meet with my shrink for the first time today. I probably get to lay on a couch and everything.

-Daniel

———

"Well hey there!" I walk into an office in the building across from the hospital, and I'm surprised to see Dr. Hannah. "I had an opening and your parents are quick. It looks like I'm officially your new therapist! How great is that?"

"*So* great..." I look around his room and instantly break out in a sweat. Exercise balls and rainbow carpets decorate the floor of his office. His desk is lime green, which stands out against the bright yellow walls. Chaos. The whole room is in chaos.

"Oh, don't worry Daniel. We will not be meeting in this room. This is where I meet with my younger clients. Follow me, good sir." He pulls his long hair into a ponytail and walks through a set of French doors that lead into a different room.

This room, in contrast to the first room, is done in neutral colors and leather furniture. Cream-colored curtains fell from the ceiling to the floor over the windows.

"For future reference, we will be meeting in here, and you can come in through that door over there." He points to a big mahogany door at the opposite side of the room. The books on the shelves are all arranged from tallest to shortest, on three different wall-length shelves. Everything feels balanced and has a place. I like it in here. It's calming. "Have a seat."

"Thanks." I push the hair out of my eyes and take a seat. One. Two. Three. Four.

"Are your parents here?"

"No, I drove myself."

"I see."

"Is that a problem?"

"No, not at all," he says. "I usually like talking to parents on the first session. But no biggie."

"Oh, sorry."

"Next week try to bring a parent, if possible, please."

"Sure."

"Great." There's that big stupid smile again. "Well, the last time I saw you was in the hospital, and since then, you have started school again. How has that been?"

"Fine, I guess."

"Just fine? Has it been a bit strange going back to school after everything that has happened?"

"That can't be helped."

"No, you're right. It doesn't mean that you still don't have some feelings about it all."

"My girlfriend broke up with me, and my best friend has been treating me like nothing even happened. It's weird."

"Sorry to hear that. It's a lot of stuff to deal with, high school is hard enough as it is."

"Yeah."

"Were you and your girlfriend really close?"

It stings more than I thought it would. "We dated for three years. I had to find out through Garrett that she dumped me."

"Garrett?"

"My best friend. I'm not even sure if he is my best friend

anymore. He never came to see me."

"Yeah, that's rough. A lot of people are afraid of hospitals. I wouldn't hold it against him. Have you decided on a college?"

My heart jumps. "I did, but I don't think they will accept me now. My GPA dropped, and nobody wants the crazy kid. I'm sure I've lost some of my scholarships already."

"Think positive! I think you should still pursue the school you want. It wouldn't hurt to have a backup plan. I think it's great that you still are planning on going to college."

"Yeah."

"I don't know if you remember our last conversation or not, but we were just getting into your relationship with your stepdad." He clicks his pen.

I forgot that I told him that.

"I want to try and deal with the root of your OCD and anxiety. A good place to start is learning how to control your behaviors before they control you. I want you to be aware that the stressors and feelings you feel around your rituals are very valid and real, but they don't have to take over every aspect of your life. You're far too precious for that!"

Now I wish my mom was here. I tap my fingers on my sternum to the beat of my heart in sets of four.

"You're anxious. That's normal for a first-time therapy session. Or in your case, it's been many years. We will start out slow—"

"On second thought, you're right, I should have brought my mom." I stand up.

"It's okay, she's given us written permission—"

"I'm really sorry." I rush to the mahogany door and nearly jog out of his office, straight to the parking lot and dive into my car, locking it behind me.

I thought I could do this, but I can't. Not today.

## December 18

I managed to survive another therapy session without walking out of it. I thought Dr. Hannah would be mad at me for freaking out last time, but he wasn't. He's one of the most relaxed people I've ever met. He said it's the antidepressants he's on. It was his attempt at a joke. It didn't make me laugh.

This last session he brought up imagining a stop sign popping up in front of me every time negative thoughts swirl around my head. He said that I have ultimate control over my body. I find it hard to believe when I can't control my compulsions most of the time. Or the stupid rituals. I don't know why I still do those. It's embarrassing.

Last night Garrett texted and told me some of the soccer team were going to crash Lauren's birthday party. I don't think they're expecting me to show up... but I really need to get out of this house. The air's too thick. I can't breathe.

-Daniel

I slowly walk down the stairs and pause at the second step from the bottom. Logic tells me that stepping on it won't make a difference. But my brain still won't let me go through with the action, so I jump over it instead.

"Hi sweetheart, how are you feeling?" Mom looks up from her canvas in the living room in front of the big window.

"That's pretty." The field of poppy flowers stands out against the neutral colors of our living room. The oranges and reds look as if they're swaying in the wind.

"Thank you. It's for a client. I hope they like it."

"Why wouldn't they? You're good."

"Well, you know, art's subjective. Want to join me? I have an extra canvas."

"No, about that… a bunch of soccer guys were invited to Lauren's birthday party. It's at her house, her parents are there. Her dad's a cop… so nothing weird would happen."

She sighs. "When is her party?"

"Today…"

Mom sets down her paintbrush and turns around to look me square in the face. "Under any other circumstances, you know I would say yes. But I'm not sure if you're ready for something like that yet. I wouldn't be there to keep an eye on you. What if you have another breakdown or panic attack?"

"I'm feeling a lot better now. I'm fine, Mom. Garrett's going to be there too if that helps."

"Not really."

I know arguing about it won't do anything. I've lived long enough to know once Mom makes up her mind, that's it. Though I'm starting to think it's a hindrance.

"What?" Mom asks. "You're clenching your fists like you're about to enter a boxing ring."

"Oh." I look down at my hands and quickly release them.

"I'm sorry you're upset about not going, but you need more time to refocus."

"Refocus?" How can she not see that I am focused? *Too* focused. So focused that I know where every book in my room is, where every line on the school floors goes. I know how hard and for how long I can scrub my own body before it goes raw. I know that even that knowledge doesn't always stop me. What the hell am I supposed to refocus on? I need a distraction. I need to feel like I'm seventeen.

"Yes. Your OCD has gotten out of control again. I'm worried about you. I honestly don't think you can handle being around a bunch of kids right now. I'm afraid it'll overwhelm you. Just, humor me and take it easy over Christmas break. After a few more therapy sessions under your belt, maybe you'll feel more confident."

"I'll feel more confident?"

"Maybe I'll... me. Maybe *I* will feel more confident in letting you go. You scared me, sweetie." She pushes away a tear.

The wind finishes deflating from my sails. "Yeah, sure. I'll stay here." I allow her to hug me. She smells like sandalwood and turpentine.

"Thank you." She gives me one more squeeze before letting me go. "I need to get this finished today, though." She picks the paintbrush back up and wets the bristles. "You sure you don't want to join me?"

"I think I'm going to make something to eat." I can't remember the last time I've sat and painted with her. I think I was five. Maybe six.

"Oh, if you're going into the kitchen, make me some tea please?" She smiles.

"Sure, Mom." I drag my feet into the kitchen and wash my hands. This is going to be a long and boring break.

## January 12

I was right. This has been the longest, most boring break in my life. Dad's been scarce. Mom's been painting. The only time I've left the house is for a therapy session with Dr. Hippie. Even that hasn't been often because he's been out of town for Christmas.

Mom and Dad thought it was a good idea to try and spend one last Christmas together. It was shit. They didn't say one word to each other, and I was too stressed out to say much. Dad left in a huff. We still haven't opened presents, but I don't know if I want to now. I would rather forget that December twenty-fifth happened. It ended with me in a ritual cycle in my room and taking a long enough shower I drained the hot water tank. It didn't help me feel better.

-Daniel

I stare at the clock in Dr. Hannah's office as the minute hand goes around. Ten more minutes. I don't want to talk anymore about my childhood. I run my fingers along the arm of the leather couch. I wonder how many people have sat on this couch? The thought causes a sensation of dust to build up between my fingers. I drop my hands into my lap and glance around for the nearest source of water and soap.

"And how are your parents?" Dr. Hannah asks as he shifts in his chair.

Good. Change of subject. "It's weird, my parents have been so absent and stuck doing their own thing. I mean I'm glad they have their own things to do, but I'm used to them being more...involved, or interested in me. I don't know what I'm doing wrong."

"Daniel, none of this is your fault. None of this is on you! You are carrying the weight of the world on your shoulders and it doesn't even belong there! Have you talked to your parents about how you're feeling?" Dr. Hannah asks.

"Of course not. How could I? It would make them feel terrible. And what would it change? Nothing, nothing at all. They hate each other. They can't even stand being in the same room. I don't know why, they won't even talk about it. I should have been better. I should have been better. I should ha—"

"No, not at all. Nothing you do or say can stop something that has been set into motion by someone else. All you can do is control yourself and your own actions. Do you understand?"

"I thought Dad would stay because he was so proud of me. I feel worthless. I'm worthless." I catch my breath and hold my fist to my forehead, trying to resist the urge to get up and leave. "So now what? I'm just screwed up for the rest of my life-life-now? All because I can't handle my parents' divorce and let my OCD spiral out of control? Because I wasn't good enough for them to work it out? Maybe they are divorcing because of my OCD..."

"You can't think like that. OCD is something that has always been there, it may even be genetic to some extent. Right now we need to work on your need for perfection." He writes down a couple of notes and watches me for a minute.

I look away and stare at my hands. I touched my hands to my head, and now my face is dirty.

"I hate to do this to you buddy, but our time is about up. For next week, I really want you to find something positive that's happening in your life right now. If you can't find it, then make it. You have a lot of good happening too, and sometimes when everything feels, or is, so negative, it can be good to find something bright and shiny to hold onto. Practice trying to resist acting on your irrational urges, too. The thoughts will always be there, the need for you to act on them will always be there. You just practice saying no. The beauty of this world is found in its imperfections. Keep journaling. Just say no. Try to counter it with something positive. We will dig deeper into your need for perfection concerning your dad next week."

"Yeah, thank you." I'm not ready to go. I don't know how to resist.

"See you soon. Please call me if you're struggling."

## January 13

I have to meet with the guidance counselor today to go over my grades from last quarter to see what I need to do to keep up my GPA. I hate that it's come to this. Although, I guess I should be grateful for the help. But it's still embarrassing.

-Daniel

## January 20

At this point I can't tell if I'm avoiding Kayla, or if she's avoiding me. I need to talk to her today, maybe I can fix this. Maybe we can stay together. I need a lifeline right now, anything. Maybe this can be my positive.

-Daniel

I drop my math books off in my locker. Another class I'm struggling in that I've never had a problem with before.

Kayla walks around the corner and freezes before turning around.

"Wait!" My mouth opens before my brain kicks in. I run after her and grab her elbow.

She looks up at me, eyes wide.

"Sorry..." I quickly drop her arm and cross mine over my chest as my anxiety slowly rises to a boiling point. "Can we talk?"

"About what?" Her tone is sharp.

"About us—"

"There isn't anything to talk about." She squeezes her textbook closer to her chest, like she's expecting a blow.

I take a step back. "Why did you dump me? Why didn't you come and talk to me first?"

"I don't want to talk about this now—"

"Don't I get a say in any of this?" My voice is louder than I anticipated. I clench my fists, trying to get myself to calm down and lower my voice. "Shouldn't I get a say, too?"

"No, Daniel, you don't. You lied to me!" she shouts. "You have all this crap to deal with all of a sudden and I can't handle it. I'm only seventeen—what do you expect me to do?"

"I didn't lie—"

"You didn't tell me, and that's the same thing. A girl should know what she's getting into when she starts dating someone."

One-two-three-four—

"And now you're freaking out. Do you know how I know that? Because you are tapping your fingers over your heart. I bet you can't even hear me talking right now." She cocks her head to the side and drills a death stare into my chest.

Dammit, stop it, Daniel. "No, I can hear you, I'm listening."

"I can't be with you right now. I'm sorry. Deal with your crap, maybe try to act normal again, then we can talk." She turns to walk away.

"Will you stop already, Kayla? This is stupid, talk to me."

"If you don't leave me alone, so help me, Daniel, I will scream."

I take another step back and shove my hands into my pockets.

She marches off, leaving me standing in the hallway with about a dozen other eyes that witnessed the whole scene.

I don't know what to do. My body can't move, anxiety is keeping me frozen in the middle of the hallway. I'm losing the inward battle that's raging inside me as I fight to keep my hands in my pockets so I don't pound it out on my chest. Four times. I need to pound my chest four times-one, two, three, four times. It's stupid, four times.

Control yourself Daniel. Why the hell am I talking to myself in third person now?

"Hey, that was brutal. Come on, let's go." Garrett walks up behind me and pushes me towards the boys' locker room. As soon as we arrive behind the safety of the heavy metal door, I rush over to the fourth sink to wash my hands. But there are only three soap dispensers. Someone took the fourth one down. Where did the fourth dispenser go? Is this some kind of joke? How can I wash my hands if there isn't a fourth soap dispenser?

My dilemma must have been obvious, because Garrett speaks up. "Man, I'm sorry. We can go to the bathroom down the hall if you want."

Panic. Panic. Panic. Panic. "Uh. No, no, no-dammit. I'm okay." I start counting to four and tapping on my chest with each count as I lean my forehead against the mirror.

"I saw that whole thing with Kayla. Do you want to talk about it?"

"What's there to talk about? She thinks I'm a freak. She doesn't want to be with a freak, and a freak is what I am. And why would you care anyway? It's not like you've been there for me. You left me to deal with this shit on my own. It's not like I can help it. I can't, I want to. I know the shit I do doesn't make sense. I hate it. It's stupid, but I feel like I have to do it, even if it confuses everyone else around me. I have to do it. It-it-it-it-dammit!" I sit on the bench and place my face in my hands.

"Look, you're right. I haven't been there. Mostly because I didn't know what to do, or what to say. Hospitals fucking scare me. I'm sorry I've been a sucky friend. I don't know what to do."

"I don't either, man."

Garrett lets out a deep sigh and sits beside me. "But you've been a pretty shitty friend too. You could have always called or texted when you needed help. Instead of all this fuckery and always running to Kayla. Who is clearly really shitty and immature."

"Ha. Who knew."

"I knew." A smug smile creeps up across his face.

"Shut up." I lightly punch him in the arm.

"You know I did."

"Yeah." I hate that he's right.

"Are you feeling better? You know we're going to walk into English class late now. All eyes are going to be on us."

"Uh. Maybe we could stay in here?"

"Have I told you that you're my best friend lately?" Garrett's grin grows wider.

"Shut up."

"Ha. Yeah."

I sheepishly look at my friend. "Actually, maybe we can go to that other restroom…"

## January 24

I wanted to kill myself today. I was embarrassed that the thought popped into my head, so I pushed it out as fast as I could. I don't really want to talk about it. It's just that I couldn't stop washing my hands. I left the house six times before I gave up and stayed home. It's stupid. I know washing my hands a hundred times isn't going to help me. I couldn't remember if I locked the front door, so I kept going back... But every time I touched the door handle, I had to go back in and wash my hands. After I finally managed to pull myself away from the sink, I would leave, lock the door, walk down the steps, then have to turn and check the lock again, starting the whole process over again.

This needs to end. I can't live like this. It's impossible to lead a normal life. It's dehumanizing. I'm a damn machine. What I don't understand is, how did I turn into this? I thought we got to the bottom of it in my therapy sessions. So why doesn't it stop? I hate it. I hate it. I hate it. I hate it.

-Daniel

**February 2**

My current assignment from Dr. Hannah: to practice control, by not fighting my impulses and allowing them to happen. He said people deal with their OCD differently, and he wants me to give in to my impulse, take a deep breath, then say that's enough and walk away from the sink... Or shower.

It sounds nuts to me, that the thought of giving in could be okay, but he says it'll help put the power back in my hands, because I would be allowing it, then I would be stopping it. Instead of fighting it until my ears bleed. I don't know if I can do that. I don't know if I'm strong enough.

I don't know.

-Daniel

———

It's Saturday morning, and neither of my parents is here. This is becoming my new normal, and I don't like it. I drop myself onto the overstuffed leather couch in Dad's office. A stack of folded boxes sticks out from behind his desk.

Someone bangs on the kitchen door. I jump up to check. Mom either locked herself out or—

"Hey, Garrett."

"Feed me." Garrett pushes his way through the door and walks straight to the fridge to pull out leftovers from last night's dinner. He opens the container, grabs a wooden spoon out of the ceramic vase near the stove, and piles food into his mouth.

This was normal once upon a time. But he stopped coming

over as often when I started dating Kayla.

I pull out a bottle of water from the lower fridge door and prop it up next to him on the counter while he stuffs his face.

"Thank you." Garrett spits out around a mouth full of mac and cheese.

"No problem." I lean against the counter and cross my arms, eyeing the new mess in front of me.

He shoves a mouthful of green beans into his mouth with his fingers.

After Garrett finishes off the green beans, he tosses the empty container into the sink and chugs the bottle of water.

"You missed one." I pull a half-eaten lemon pie out of the fridge and place it on the counter in front of Garrett.

"Fuck." His eyes grow wide. "You know the way to my heart." He grabs a clean spoon from a nearby drawer and takes two huge bites of the pie. "Shit, this is so good. Your mom make it?"

I nod. Garrett's mom doesn't cook. Hell, she hardly even goes grocery shopping. Once when we were eight, Garrett stayed the night. I thought he was going to eat us out of house and home, so I called him a pig. He looked so ashamed after, I wanted to punch myself in the face for being an asshole. Mom scolded me and told me to never judge a hungry child because they don't always know where their next meal will come from. It's always been like that with him. My family's taken care of Garrett for as long as I can remember. And he's always taken care of me. Until I ditched him for Kayla. I was an idiot.

"What? You lookin' like you're going to hug me or something." Garrett shoots me an uncomfortable look.

"Remember when we were younger and you lived with us for a few months?"

"Yeah, it was the best few months of my life, followed by the worst few months of my life in foster care. I hated your parents for so long afterwards, because I thought it was their fault."

"I thought I was the luckiest kid on the planet because I had a brother. It felt like you lived here for years."

Garrett smiles. "Yeah, well, I'll always be your brother. Unless you date another Kayla. But don't worry, I'll cut off your balls before you make that mistake again."

"Noted..." I cringe. "So, why are you here?"

"I was hungry."

"Okay..."

"Can't a guy stop by and say hi to his brother?" Garrett finishes off the lemon pie.

"Yeah, of course. Usually you text first."

"I lost my phone."

"Sucks."

Awkward silence.

Garrett dumps the rest of the dirty dishes in the sink. I wish he would put them in the dishwasher. It's right there next to the sink. I cross my arms and pull them tight across my chest. If I go and clean everything now, I'm just going to look like an asshole.

"It's just weird trying to talk to you about stuff again," Garrett blurts out.

"Seriously? Just tell me." It came out more annoyed than I was expecting. The food crumbs on the counter are staring at me.

"I think I'm going to ask Sara to senior prom." He sucks in a breath and puffs out his cheeks.

"Who?"

"New Girl? Lauren's friend? Met her in the office way back? Junior…"

"Oh. You barely know her." I haven't thought about prom. I was supposed to go with Kayla. No way could I go with anyone else. Not that anyone would go with me at this point…

"Yeah, but she seems pretty cool. I don't know, I feel like we would have a lot of fun together. Maybe get her out of her house… make her smile…"

"You like her."

"So? Yeah." A stupid smile plasters itself across Garrett's face.

"I don't think she's into you." I force myself to look away from the minor disaster in the kitchen. The little food bits in a small pile on the counter…

"Maybe. But she's who I want to ask."

"Then ask her."

"Yeah?"

"Yeah."

If it was even possible, Garrett's smile gets wider.

"Dude." I shove him off the counter. "You have a crush on New Girl."

Garrett opens up the fridge again. "It is possible, my heart's not completely made of stone." He pulls out an orange.

Orange peels. I feel my forehead crease as I shove the trash can in his direction, then head over to the sink to wash my hands. And since I'm here, I might as well load the dishwasher. I pull it open and accidentally knock my left shin on the door and automatically knock my right shin to balance myself out.

"Did you tell Kayla about your OCD before your middle-aged-woman meltdown at school?" Garrett shoves a slice of orange in his mouth to make it look like teeth.

I shake my head. I didn't need to. I had everything under control when I met her. Sure, there were a few things she noticed, like the potential for germs really bothering me. But that's because she wasn't fully aware of the possibly devastating effects germs could have on a person. I wouldn't be able to handle knowing I made her or anyone else sick because I wasn't clean. She wouldn't have been with me if I wasn't so clean.

I place the last dish into the dishwasher and wash my hands again.

"Hhmm," is all he says before he puts another orange slice into his mouth.

"What?"

"Nothing. I mean, something. You really know how to surprise a girl, that's all. There are lots of women out there that appreciate surprises. Heck, even look forward to a good surprise. You just got a bad egg. That's all."

"Shut up."

Garrett laughs. "Nah, I am sorry you guys broke up. But that's something you need to warn the person you're dating about. You know?"

I shrug. I know I screwed up.

I wash my hands again. I need to stop this. I suck in a deep breath, working myself up to step away from the sink.

"Okay, Mr. Clean. You done cleaned all the man hair off your arms." Garrett shuts the faucet off with the side of his hand and puts another slice into his mouth. "Do you still have that Nintendo?"

I smile. "Yeah."

"Well then, let's get to it so I can kick your ass like I used to."

"Shut up." He follows me into the den. Garrett's always been good at bringing me back down to earth. I didn't realize how much I missed him.

## February 4

I'm trying here. I want to get better, but I don't know how that's possible if I can't shut my damn brain off. How am I supposed to ignore my thoughts when they are screaming at me? I can't. I can't do it. I'm a failure on so many levels. This disease is going to consume me from the inside out. Soon the freak inside will be dripping from my pores and even strangers will know what I am as they walk past me. Worse than that, they will be afraid to even touch me because they will be terrified that my dripping pores will ooze out and cover them.

I'm disgusting, and it doesn't matter how many times I shower or wash my hands, the filth always seems to crawl from the ground and defile my body. I want to be clean. If I'm clean people will like me and respect me. If I'm clean people will stay. I won't be abandoned. But how can I stay clean when I can see the germs dive into my skin and swim throughout my body?

Who wants to be close to this mess?

I have abandoned myself, my own integrity. This road I am running down is full of cracks that threaten my existence. Cracks which grow into a giant noose that promises to circle my neck and cut out the lights. I am tempted to beg the rope to grow tighter.

Maybe if the oxygen gets cut off from my brain, I won't notice the numbers rushing past my eyes demanding me to count every single one. Slapping me in the face if I miss one, or wind up on the wrong number.

I thought this was supposed to get better, easier. I am really trying here. I want to get better, but I'm afraid I can't.

-Daniel

## February 9

I didn't go to school today. I wanted to go, but I can't. My heart won't stop beating a million times a second. Every time I try to take in a deep breath, it makes me dizzy. I've rearranged the books on my shelves seven times, and I still have to do it one more time. I can't leave it at seven, it has to be eight, but if I accidentally do it one more time, I have to make it twelve times. Maybe sixteen.

I was going to be late anyways, because earlier I had to take a shower. Four times. Four damn times. I need to call Dr. Hannah, but I'm afraid of what he'll say. What if I have to go back into the mental hospital? Then I won't even be in the running for salutatorian. My parents are at work, neither of them knows I'm home, but I can't call them either.

Screw this. I have to call someone.

-Daniel

"Hello?"

"Dr. Hannah?" My voice shakes, I don't know what I'm doing, or if I should be calling him.

"Yes, who's this?"

"Uh, it's Daniel, Daniel Quincy."

"Oh, hi, Daniel! Shouldn't you be at school right now?" His voice stays upbeat and doesn't waver.

"Yeah, I should be at school." Should be... can't though.

"What can I do for you, good sir?"

"I don't know. I can't stop—my heart is racing, I'm having trouble breathing. I keep trying to stop fixing my books, hoping it'll help me calm down, but I can't. I can't do it. What if something goes wrong if I don't finish it? What if I will never be able to stop?"

"Oh buddy, that's a hard place to be in. It's good that you gave me a call."

"What do I do? How can I stop?" I squeeze my eyes shut.

"Well, one thing that could help: did you take your pills this morning?"

Shit. How could I forget? I rush over to my bathroom and pull out the pill bottles from behind my mirror. Empty. The realization of my pill bottles being empty for the last month or so drops me back into reality. How could I forget to take my pills? How stupid am I?

"Hello? You still there Daniel?"

"Um, I'm out."

"What?"

"I forgot to pick up my refill yesterday," I lie. I can't remember if I've ever gotten a refill after the first prescriptions. "I can't believe I forgot. When did I start forgetting to do things? I don't just forget."

"Well, that's okay. Taking pills isn't a normal thing in your routine yet. Soon you'll get used to it. Maybe you should call your mom or dad. They can help you get your refill."

"No—I can't. They're at work, they already think I'm at school. I can't do that. I can't-can't-can't-dammit! I don't want them to worry. They already worry about me enough."

"Hmm. Well you have yourself in quite a pickle, don't you?"

"This isn't funny."

"No-no you're right. This isn't funny. Which is why you need to call one of your parents, or I will. You're still a minor, I can't keep an incident like this between us."

"Right." Damn.

"Now, do you want to call, or should I call on your behalf?"

"I can't call them." I hesitate.

"Mmkay. I am going to hang up on you now and call. Who would you like me to call?"

Who's going to freak out less? "My dad."

"Right away, sir! Hang in there, Daniel."

"Yeah."

*click*

Shit. Shit. Shit. Shit.

———

"Daniel?" Dad walks in the front door and slams it behind him. I don't answer. I can't answer. Instead I'm sitting in the middle of my bedroom floor in nothing but my boxer briefs. Why? Because the lines on my T-shirt did not match up with the stitches on the seam. The belt I was wearing only has five holes in it. Stupid. "Hey, what's going on?" Dad rushes into my room with a pharmacy bag and a sports drink.

"I can't do it. I can't live like this. Nothing makes sense. None of the lines match up and I can't wear it. I need it to be even, I need it to be perfect, but it doesn't match up." I start tapping my fingers on my chest again in intervals of four.

"Oh, Daniel." The pity drips from his eyes as he grabs my hand.

"NO! No, sorry, you can't touch me. I have to go wash my hands." I jump up and run to the bathroom sink and start scrubbing. "One, two, three, four." One... Two... Three... Four...

Dad sighs and sits down on my bed. After rubbing his eyes, he stares at me.

"I can't-can't-can't-dammit! I can't live like this. Why is this still happening to me? I don't want to be like this." Scrub harder, clean your hands, clean them. Four more times and you'll be clean.

"Daniel, come take your pills." He has tears in his eyes now. He must be really disappointed in me.

"Wait, I will. Let me finish cleaning my hands. Maybe if I'm cleaner you'll stay. Maybe if I was better you wouldn't be leaving-leaving, shit. Leaving me."

"Is that what you think I'm doing?" Tears are freely swimming down his face now.

"I thought if I was good, and got good grades, and was a good son you would stay. And you did, for a long time. But now you're leaving. What did I do that was so bad?" I force myself to stop scrubbing my hands. I grip the edges of the sink as hard as I can, to help me resist the urge of flinging my hands back under the running water. "Everything's ruined now. Everyone at school is talking about me. You've been coming home late and avoiding me. My girlfriend broke up with me because she thinks I'm a freak now. I can't do this anymore. I can't—"

"Is that what you think? You think that I am leaving you?" Dad gets up and stands in the doorway to my bathroom.

"Aren't you?" I stare at the wasted water spinning down the drain like its own miniature hurricane.

Dad reaches over and turns off the water. I can't help it, I turn the water back on, then back off, then back on, eight times until I finally pull myself away.

"Daniel." He pulls me into his chest and hugs me hard. "I am never going to abandon you. Don't ever think that. You are my son and I love you. I adopted you remember? I adopted you because I wanted YOU to be MY son. No one else. You could be the most disorganized kid on the planet who gets bad grades and sucks at soccer, and I would still love you and call you my own."

My tears flood his collared shirt. "Then why are you leaving me?"

"I will never leave you, Daniel. I will always be there when you need me. Your mother and I simply can't seem to work things out. We tried keeping it hidden from you for a very long time. But I guess if you shake a bottle enough times, it explodes regardless if you leave the lid on or not." He pushes me back so he can look at my tear-stained face. "You need to know how much I love you. I love YOU, Daniel. Having you for a son isn't something I take lightly. Please try to understand, it's not working between your mom and me—but it will always work between me and you." He squeezes me one more time. "You need to take your pills now, and I need to call work and tell them I'm not coming back today."

"I'm sorry—"

"Don't you ever apologize to me when you need help. We're a team, remember?"

"Thanks, Dad..."

"I love you, kid."

"Yeah. Love you too."

## February 10

It's amazing how long I've avoided the words 'stepdad' and 'adopted.' I don't know why I so desperately wanted to feel 'normal.' I mean, I know why, but it's embarrassing to think about why. I would rather pretend that Mom wasn't with six different men (that I remember) before she settled down with my dad. They all left. All of them. I tried being good, clean. Perfect. I thought if I were perfect, they would stay. So I tried really hard, and then Dad stayed, and he and Mom got married. It was amazing. I always did what I was told, I always kept my room clean and showered when I was supposed to. I worked really hard in school to get good grades so I could prove to him that I was worth it.

I wanted to make sure Dad stayed, so I used to stay in and read, so he could see how smart I was. I wanted him to be so proud of me, that when I found out he loved soccer, I joined soccer, and I studied soccer so I could be the best. He told me I could be president one day, so I tried being likable and became class president almost every year since junior high. Then student body president.

I did everything he ever wanted me to do because I thought that would make him stay with me and Mom forever. I let these feelings and actions rule my life for as long as I can remember, and now I'm not really sure what to do with myself now that Mom and Dad aren't going to be together anymore. I hate myself for doing that. All that pressure. But I also hate that after all of that, I still don't get the happy ending I was counting on.

-Daniel

## February 11

I am staying home today too. It's not that I don't want to go to school, but I can't get out the door. I called Dad, and he said not to worry about it. He and Mom are going to try and get off of work early today. Garrett is going to bring by my homework.

I was extra nervous today because I was supposed to be meeting with the school counselor to go over my grades and to see how else she could be helpful. I hate it. It feels like the school is starting to treat me like one of those special needs kids all of a sudden. Or one of those jocks that are too stupid to tie their shoe, but they can throw a ball at ninety miles an hour, so they 'accommodate' them just enough to help them pass.

Do they think that my IQ has dropped to mentally incapable levels all of a sudden? Is that what the whole school thinks? That I've had some massive brain trauma and now I'm too stupid to socialize or do calculus? I used to love calculus, all forms of math. I liked how everything made sense, and the numbers or letters had a purpose and they never changed. Now, I can't handle all the numbers and stupid layout of the formulas. I waste most of my time now rearranging the formulas so they are more aesthetically pleasing and symmetrical.

The most frustrating thing about having OCD is: I know that half the things I do don't make any sense. What does washing my hands a hundred and twenty-one times have to do with how much my dad loves me? Not a damn thing.

My room is the only safe place right now. Whenever I leave, my heart races and I find it hard to focus. It's safe in here.

Everything has its place, and my bathroom sink is less than four steps from my bed. I wish I never had to leave.

-Daniel

⸻

"Hey, what's up?" Garrett walks into my room and places a folder on my desk. On the corner of my desk. Not in the center, or lined up on one of the edges, but lopsided and balancing on the corner. "All your stuff from your teachers is in here. Except calculus, because I don't have that class, and I wasn't about to go in there. That teacher's creepy."

"Yeah, no worries. I can wait another day to do my math homework." I can't help myself. I get up and fix the folder, placing it even with the lines in the wood grain on my desk. "Thanks for bringing this though. I don't want to fall too far behind."

"Any time. So, are you sick today? Like—" Garrett points at his temple and moves his finger in a circular motion.

"I'm not crazy," I snap.

"No, of course you're not fucking crazy. You know what I mean."

"I have OCD."

"Fine. Did you ditch school again today because of your OCD?"

"Yeah." My face heats up and I shove my hands in the pockets of my sweats as I look out the window.

"No need to feel embarrassed, man. You have some major shit to work through. You're not going to be like this forever, are you?" He plops down on my bed, the same way he has done for as long as I can remember.

"Garrett." I let out a frustrated sigh and rub the bridge of my nose. With one finger, then the next finger, then the one after that—all five fingers. I ball my other hand in a tight fist to help fight the urge to do the same thing with my other hand. "This isn't something that I can turn off."

"You've always been a little OCD, I guess. Like if something's unbalanced you go berserk. Or how you can't ever take showers at school after practice because there are too many germs. You always have to have your things ordered and put in the right place in your room or locker. The folder I just dropped on your desk? Yeah, I get it, you're OCD, but why is this any different than before? Why is it such a big deal now?"

"You're right, I've always been weird."

"Dude, that's not what I'm trying to say."

"I don't know. I've gotten worse, it's not something I can just shut off whenever I feel like it. I want to—more than ever. I want to go back to the way I was, with keeping everything under control, but I can't. I don't understand how or why it happened like this. I just—" Breathe in, breathe out. One, two, three, four. One, two, three, four. One, two, three, four. One, two, three, four. One, two—

"You okay Daniel?" Garrett stands up and grabs the arm that is attached to the hand I am using to count and tap my fingers with.

"Uh, yeah..." I have to start over now. One, two, three...

Garrett waits patiently for me to finish.

"Sorry." My face is one big fire.

"Man, don't be sorry. I don't get what's happening in your head. I want to, but there's a certain creep factor about it that I am trying to get used to."

I am a freak. I am a freak. I am a freak. I am a freak. Dammit. "I get it. It's weird. I hate it. I'm afraid to go anywhere because of it."

"Don't be afraid. I'll knock the shit out of anyone who stares at you or calls you weird names or whatever."

"Ha. Thanks. I think…"

"Anyways, I gotta go. There is an exam tomorrow in Spanish, I need to pass or I'll fail the whole damn class. Will you be there?"

"Yeah, maybe. I don't know."

"Try. I know you got some kind of arrangement with the school about homework and tests and shit, but I am starting to miss seeing you at school. It's not the same without you there."

"Even with me now being the school freak?"

"Naw man, you are the fucking captain of the soccer team. I bet you might even be crowned king for prom. No one cares, we all have our crap. Just, be present. You're only a senior once."

That's not true. They all care. Everyone fucking cares. If they didn't, no one would whisper or laugh at me behind my back whenever I have to count something or repeat the same word over and over again when I get frustrated. "Yeah, you're right, no one cares. It's probably all in my head."

"See you tomorrow?"

"Sure, thanks for bringing my homework."

"Later."

One, two, three, four. One, two, three, four. One, two, three, four. One, two, three, four. I strip off my clothes and get in the shower. I know this is my fourth shower of the day. I know it's stupid.

## February 12

The parents are going to have me committed. I can feel their tension reaching up through the floorboards just begging to strangle me while I sleep. I've locked myself in my room for the last three days. Mom's been leaving food for me outside the door on a cooking tray. She's threatened to call Dr. Hannah several times if I keep doing this. She doesn't understand. I have to do this. I have to do this to keep them safe. What if I go out and get them sick with germs I picked up from somewhere? What if I make them crazy because of all this? They would hate me. I can't have them hate me. It wouldn't be right if they were divorced and hated me at the same time. Where would I live? They would push me back and forth until I am nothing but a worn, threadbare rug. There would be nothing left of me. Maybe that's what they want? It would be easier for everyone if I was no longer around. No one misses me at school. Hardly anyone comes over or texts me anymore. I want to blame them. I want to hate them, but I can't, because I know this is my fault. Who wants to be around a freak anyway? I can barely stand being around myself.

I have to shower again, I need to. I need to be clean, but Dad threatened to turn the water off if he heard the shower running again. Dr. Hannah said it's supposed to help with my rehabilitation if my parents don't give in to my compulsions. I'll just have to wait until after they go to sleep, then Dad won't know, and I can be clean. Doesn't he want me to be clean??

-Daniel

It's 2:00 a.m. I am pretty sure everyone is dead asleep, so I quickly take off all my clothes and get in the shower. Hot scalding water shoots at me, aiming to kill every microorganism on my skin. I grab the soap, pour it over my body, and rake the scrub brush against every inch of me. Over and over and over again. One, two, three, four. One, two, three, four. One, two, three, four. One, two—

The water suddenly shuts off, leaving me standing alone in my shower only half-rinsed. Red marks cover my body from my attempts to pull the top layer of skin off.

NO-NO-NO-NO!

The bang on my bedroom door lets me know that whatever is about to come next is not going to be pleasant. I stay frozen in the shower.

"Daniel? What are you doing?" Dad walks into my room and stops before he makes it to my open bathroom door.

"Turn the water back on. I'm not finished, I'm not even rinsed, please turn it back on!"

"No. Get out." He's pissed.

"I am not getting out of this damn shower until you turn the water back on." Is he joking? I'm disgusting. I need to finish washing.

"How many showers have you had today? Are you going to pay the water bill? Come on, get out, and go to bed." He walks into the bathroom, pulls back the shower door and pushes a towel in my face. "What the hell, Daniel?" His eyes grow wide as he examines the red marks across my chest.

"I need to finish showering. Please, Dad, turn the water back on!"

"No, we're getting you out now. Don't give in to this, Daniel! Be strong. Come on—"

"NO! Go to hell and turn the damn water back on! Turn it on!" I don't mean a word that is barreling out of my mouth. I hate myself for it. Why am I reacting like this?

"This isn't you. I know this is not you talking, but I'm sorry, Son, I can't do that. You have to fight this compulsion." He wraps the towel around me and tries to pull me out of the shower. Shooting pain flows through my jaw like electricity as I try my hardest to keep my mouth shut. All I want to do is word vomit a string of profanities at him. Why do I want to do that? He's right. I know he's right.

"Please, just turn the water back on, I won't take a long shower, I promise-please, Dad. You don't understand—" Shit. Shit. Shit—

"No. Now come on."

I lose control and collapse to the floor. I hate myself for the heat that's radiating from my damn face. What is wrong with me? Dad's right, this isn't me at all. The words keep flowing uncontrollably. I try tapping my fingers to gain some sort of self-control, but instead I begin to beat my chest with my fist. "One, two, three, four." Four times, I count to four as I try to reach my heart through my sternum.

Dad sits on the carpet quietly and waits for me to stop. The silence is long and uncomfortable. I want nothing more than for the floor to suck me in through its cracks so I can join the darkness below.

Finally, a short stint of relief flows over me. "Dad…"

"It's okay, you don't have to say anything." He pats me on the back and I pretend to ignore the billions of germs that now cover me.

"No, I do. I don't know why I acted like that. I'm so sorry. I don't understand. I lost control and it was stupid..." I'm so ashamed. What an idiot. None of that makes sense. My skin stings where I scrubbed too hard. Dammit. I look down at my arms which are now glowing red from my attempts to get clean.

"Get ready for bed. I'm going to stay in here tonight." He grabs the extra blanket at the foot of my bed and goes to lay down on the long window bench under my bedroom window.

"You don't have to—"

"I want to."

"Dad, I am sorry."

"I know. Good night, Daniel."

"Yeah. Good night. I really am sorry."

"Good night."

## February 13

I don't know how to explain the relief I have right now. I feel secure in my relationship with my dad. At the same time, I still feel out of control, and I hate feeling like that. I want to go back to the way things were, when I wasn't so 'OCD' or whatever. I know the switch flipped when I found out about my parents' divorce, but why can't I switch it back off?

-Daniel

## February 20

I feel embarrassed for writing this down, but only because I'm sure no one else would understand this. It's been obvious for most of my life that I have a germ aversion. People on the outside think it's because I am a germaphobe.

But on the inside, if I touch something that's covered in germs, my anxiety rises to explosive levels. My hands feel thick and dry, like I'm wearing old gardening gloves filled with mud. The skin on my arms itch as the sensation of a thousand germs entering my body leaves tiny holes all over my skin.

When I feel like that, and I can't wash my hands right away, I feel like I'm going to die. I can't focus or concentrate. Sometimes it takes multiple washes until the thick muddy gloves go away. There are days when I feel like they will never go away and I walk around with dust settled all over my skin, so I avoid touching other people so I don't get them covered as well.

None of this is logical or makes sense. I get that. But why does this happen to me?

-Daniel

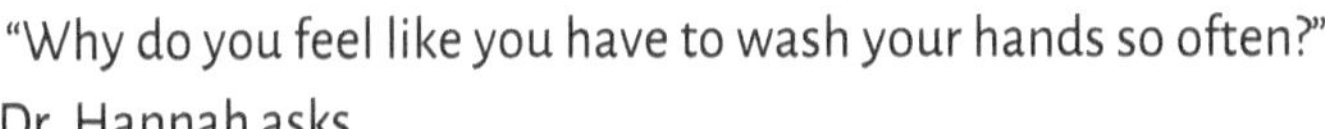

"Why do you feel like you have to wash your hands so often?" Dr. Hannah asks.

"Because I don't want to be dirty."

"Say I dropped my notebook on the floor, and I picked it back up right away and tried to shake your hand, would I then be dirty?"

"Yes."

"Why?"

"Because you picked up germs off the floor."

Dr. Hannah drops his notebook on the floor, then picks it up. Shit. I know what's coming next.

"Come shake my hand, Daniel."

"Nope." What is he doing?

"It's part of the exercise. You used to be able to shake hands. Don't you want to do that again?"

"No, I think I'm fine." I'm not grabbing his hand.

"What do you think will happen if you shake my hand?"

"I would get dirty."

"What would happen if you got dirty?" He clicks his pen three times. Only three times. Why only three? Why at all?

"I could get sick."

"What happens if you get sick?"

"I would be disgusting and covered in germs."

"What would happen if you were disgusting?"

"Is this necessary?" Seriously. My head throbs.

"Yep. Now, what would happen if you were disgusting?"

"I could get my parents sick from all the germs."

"What would happen if your parents get sick?"

I stare at the plain tan carpet on the floor. I really don't like this.

"Take your time."

"They would be disappointed in me—disappointed that I got them sick because I didn't wash my hands." A sigh escapes from my chest.

"What would happen if they were disappointed in you?" He keeps pushing.

"My dad would get angry."

"Then what?"

"He might not like me after that."

"And?"

I rub the back of my neck, trying to ignore the sinking feeling in the pit of my stomach.

"And?" he patiently repeats again.

"I don't know..." This is stupid.

"Take your time, I think you do know."

Time? I don't have time. I don't know what he wants from me. Does he need me to admit how much of a freak I already know I am? I know none of this makes sense. It's not logical. It's shitty and stupid.

"Do you think if your dad doesn't like you, he will do something? Maybe something negative?"

"Maybe." One, two, three, four. One, two—

"Why are you counting?"

I look down at my chest. My chest that holds my heart—a heart that's threatening to stop at any minute due to the anxiety that is swelling up from the floor, promising to swallow me whole.

"I-I don't know why I'm counting. It just helps I guess."

"Helps with what?"

"It helps me feel better. Counting helps me refocus. When I was younger Mom would make me breathe in and out four seconds at a time whenever I got upset to help me calm down."

"Those are good skills to have."

"Yeah."

"Now, back to your dad. What would happen if your dad didn't like you anymore?"

The forced air from my lungs feels more like shards of glass. "If he didn't like me anymore, that means he would leave me, and if he left me that would mean he doesn't love me, and if he doesn't love me then I'm not worth it—I'm not worth staying around for—like all those other guys before him—they left. They left me behind after all those empty, hollow promises of sticking around and being my dad. He's just like the rest of them. He's a liar! He promised he would stay, he promised he would love me forever and be my dad. Now he's leaving and I'm not going to have a dad anymore! I'm disgusting. I don't blame him, who would want the product of a one-night stand anyway?" Shit. I thought I worked through this already. I hold my breath to keep in the few tears that were threatening to slip out of my eyes. "I'm going to be alone. I feel so worthless."

"What about your mom? Do you think she values you?"

"Sure, she loves me, but it's not the same."

"Daniel, I want you to know: everything that you are feeling is valid. Your emotions are a real thing—that is real fear you are dealing with. However, do you think it's true?"

"Of course not, it's stupid. He already told me he wouldn't stop loving me. He's been my dad for a long time. He wouldn't leave me behind after he promised he wouldn't leave me behind. Would he?"

"I have seen the way your dad looks at you—with great pride in his eyes! Your origins, where you came from, or what you're a product of doesn't matter. You are someone very special and worth loving! You are NOT defective, or broken, or stupid, or disgusting. You will NOT be abandoned. You are NOT worthless. Have you talked to your dad about these feelings?"

"Yeah." Dr. Hannah is a very passionate man. I can't decide if

I like or feel awkward around the hippie vibe he sends out.

He reaches his hand out towards me. "Shake it."

Dammit.

"Come on, it's not going to bite you."

I hesitantly reach out and grab his hand with my sweaty palm.

"See? That wasn't so bad." He smiles and drops my hand. I watch a hundred million microorganisms crawl into my skin. "Now, how are you feeling?"

"I really need to wash my hand."

"Need to? Or want to?"

"I want to..." I stare down at the muddy garden gloves clinging to my skin.

"Why?"

"Because I feel filthy."

"But I'm not filthy." He furrows his eyebrow like I hurt his feelings.

That's debatable. Who knows what's growing in that long ponytail of his?

"I showered this morning. I washed my hands before our appointment. I haven't done anything to make my hands unclean. Do you still feel the need to wash your hands?"

"Yes."

"Even after we just talked about your reasoning behind the need to constantly wash your hands isn't true? That it doesn't make sense?"

He makes sense. I know it's stupid. Shit. Shit. Shit. "Shit."

"What?"

"Uh. Sorry."

"You can't help the feelings you are experiencing. You can't stop the thoughts from popping up into your head. BUT, let me tell you what you can do Daniel." He leans forward like he's about to tell me some great secret. "You can choose not to act on those thoughts and compulsions you are having. Isn't that great news?"

I stare at him. Does he think I'm dumb? If it were that easy, wouldn't I have stopped already?

"It's true. For instance. Right now you are fighting the urge to run down the hall to the little boys' room so you can wash your hands. Am I right?"

I stare at him until he makes his point.

"The same self-control and will power you are using right now needs to be used in your day to day life. It's not going to be easy, in fact, it's going to be really difficult at times. You need to make sure you have a strong support system set up around you. Make sure your friends and your family know to not let you indulge in these compulsions, but to help you stop them in their tracks. You think you can do that? Talk to your friends about this?"

"No." Why would I do that? Hey dude, whenever I can't stop washing my hands, could you do me a favor and tackle me to the disgusting bathroom floor if I don't stop the first time? No. Freaking. Way.

"Try."

"I can try."

"Great! Well, that is your homework for the week: don't give in to the compulsions! Resist, my friend, and set your mind free!" Dr. Hannah stands up and opens the door with his hand out to shake mine. "See you next time."

"Yeah, sure." I look at his hand, and back at his face as I

nervously walk past him and down the hall without looking back.

I'm not going to wash my hands. I'm not going to wash my hands. I'm not going to wash my hands. I'm not going to wash my hands... Dammit.

## February 21

The fact that everything negative happening in my life is connected to my fear of being abandoned by Dad is crazy. Is it completely crazy though? I can't be perfect enough even if I try. It's stupid. I've thought about what Dr. Hannah said... The possibility of hope, that this is something I can control, or stop in its tracks makes everything feel more manageable. If he's right, that means my OCD doesn't make me crazy, and it doesn't have to ruin my life. The downside is, it also may be something I will have to keep in check for the rest of my life. I knew this was a possibility from when I was younger, but I really thought it would go away.

Whenever I get frustrated, whenever I feel overwhelmed, whenever a tense situation pops up, I have to keep myself in check. I wish this was something that could just go away. I want life to go back to normal. It feels like I'm going to be stuck in a constant circle for the rest of my life.

I read a statistic today saying that sixty percent of people who have severe OCD end their lives in suicide. Is that going to be me? Is my life going to get so out of control that I'll just end it?

-Daniel

## March 1

It's soccer season. My school is so huge the girls usually play soccer in the fall and the guys in the spring, but we've always been able to still practice with the girls during the fall, and them with us in the spring. Even though it's always been my favorite time of year, I've been in leagues since I was five, the excitement is almost overshadowed by the ball of anxiety threatening to consume my body at any given moment. I want to play, but I wonder if it would be smarter to back out? There were scouts at one of our big games last year, and one of them told me he was looking forward to seeing me play my senior year. This will only end in disappointment. How else would it end with the current trajectory my life is on?

-Daniel

"All right guys, I'm the new soccer coach this year, you can call me Coach Tiegs. A little about myself: I played professional soccer in Europe for four years, until I broke and destroyed my ankle. Don't think that means you can get off easy, I can still do a little running and keep up with you kids." He smiles and shifts his clipboard in his hands. "You guys voted, and your team captain this year is Garrett Hunter, and co-captain is Daniel Quincy. Why don't we start with a few laps around the field."

Co-captain? When did I get demoted?

"Hey, sorry about that Daniel, it came as a surprise to me too but... the guys wanted someone more..."

"Not crazy?"

Garrett grabs and squeezes my shoulders. "Don't say that."

"Did you guys keep me on as co-captain as a pity gesture?"

"Dude, I can't captain alone, I need you. The guys just wanted you to feel like you still fit in. Not in the you're-the-weird-kid sort of way... Just that we all support you and want you to get better."

"Get better, huh?" He doesn't get it. I start counting my steps in groups of four while running on the outside edge of the field. This is not how I thought this season would go.

## March 3

One. Two. Three. Four.
One. Two. Three. Four.
One. Two. Three. Four.
One. Two. Three. Four.
One. Two. Three. Four.
One. Two. Three. Four.
One. Two. Three. Four.
One. Two. Three. Four.

-Daniel

## March 5

First game today. I don't know if I'm ready. I've never been this nervous over a soccer game before. But part of me wishes I came down with the flu. Metaphorically, of course.

-Daniel

The roar of the crowd reaches into the locker room. The coach comes in to give us a last pep talk before we head out to the field, but I don't hear it. My brain is too loud. The team we are playing against has been state champions for the last two years in a row. They're good. And there are a lot of people out there right now.

"You got this." Garrett gives me a fist bump. "This isn't your first rodeo."

"Yeah, don't fuck it up," Jace comments as he walks past me.

I'm taking it as a good sign that he's even talking to me.

"Hey look, we're all friends again." Garrett grins.

"Hilarious." I pull in a deep breath. My insides are vibrating. I love soccer. I love the adrenaline that comes when I play. This isn't that big of a deal.

After getting pepped up we run out to the field, but I freeze before we hit the grass. The field is brand new turf, alternating every yard with dark green and lighter green fake grass, across the whole field. That's where I force my focus to stay, but it doesn't. Looking up, hundreds of people fill the stands surrounding the field. This is what happens when one huge school plays against another giant school. People, lots of people.

Shit. Shit. Shit. Shit.

The rest of the team pushes past me before Garrett turns and comes back for me. "What's up? You're starting, come on!"

"I—" I freeze again. How do I explain to my best friend and captain of the soccer team that I can't walk on that field? An anchor sits in my chest, keeping me from moving forward.

"Come on." He grabs the front of my jersey and pulls me onto the field.

One-two-three-four. Dammit.

We flip a coin and I take my position at midfield. This is fine. I just need to focus. I rub my already sweaty palms onto my shorts and pull up my socks.

"Back up, Daniel, attack position. You got this man!" Garrett shouts.

My parents' cheers float above the crowd. My name floats from the stands. I find them waving and cheering. That's good, they're together. My heart slows down a bit. At least they can agree on one thing, coming to my games. Even if they are in separate cars.

"You awake, Daniel?" Jace yells at me from behind.

"Yeah, sorry." I move forward a few feet. This is going to suck.

The game starts. I try to get back into the right mindset, but I can't. A guy runs right past me and makes a goal. It happened so fast, I didn't hear the whistle blow.

"Come on! What the hell are you doing?" Jace yells again.

"Do you need to wait this one out? What's going on? This isn't like you." Garrett's frustration is evident.

I look over to where my parents are, their faces full of concern and confusion. I'm such a disappointment. I shouldn't be here. Everyone is disappointed in me. Probably even embarrassed. I can't play soccer anymore. What the hell was I thinking? "I have to go." I turn and run off the field, passing the coach back into the locker room where I take my cleats off and throw them at a locker. Tears burn down my face as I drop to the bench. I'm such an idiot.

The coach comes in after me. "What's going on? Are you all right? Do you feel sick or something?"

"No, no I'm fine-fine-fine-fine-dammit! I'm okay, I can't go back out there."

"Why not? What's going on? If you don't feel well, at least come support your team from the bench."

"I can't—"

"Daniel? Are you all right, honey?" Mom and Dad rush into the locker room.

"He's fine, just a little stage fright." The coach now seems annoyed.

Great, now he hates me. I'll add him to my growing list of disappointed people. "Mom, can you take me home?"

"Of course, honey. Get your things." She doesn't hesitate.

"He doesn't need to go home, he needs to support the team—he's co-captain. Daniel, what's going on?" The coach gets down on his knee to look me in the eyes.

Dad crosses his arms over his chest and stares at me. "Did you bring your pills with you?"

I tap my fingers on my chest while counting to four, four times before I can answer. "I didn't think it would be that big of a deal. How was I supposed to know this would happen? It's not supposed to happen like this." A loud roar from the crowd explodes into the locker room. Shouts of joy float in from the crowd. Someone must have scored. I really hope it was us.

"You should always be prepared," Dad says.

"I'm sorry." My face heats up.

The coach butts in. "Pills for what?"

"Nothing."

"Honey..." Mom pushes.

"I have OCD, it's not a big deal. Why are we always making this a big deal?"

"Well, it's not a *big* deal, but it's a deal that's taken over a bit right now. You should have brought your anxiety meds." Mom sits beside me.

"OCD? Like you're afraid of germs and stuff? Is that a thing?" The couch butts in again.

"Maybe you should look it up, Coach, it can be a debilitating condition," Dad spits out.

"Oh, I'm sorry." He stands up really fast and whispers to my parents. "I had no idea. I wasn't trying to be offensive."

I lose it, I can't help the emotions coming over me. I stand up and grab my bag and cleats. Then I immediately drop them and walk over to the row of sinks behind the lockers, find the fourth one and wash my hands. Over, and over, and over again.

"Come on Daniel, let's go home." Dad tries to calm me down as he reaches for me.

"Leave me alone! I'm fine."

"Well, I will let you two deal with Daniel, I need to get back out there..." The coach grabs his clipboard and slowly backs out of the locker room as the crowd erupts in another cheer.

Mom gathers my things and takes a seat on the bench closest to me.

"One, two, three, four. One, two, three, four. One, two, three, four. One, two, three, four." More soap, four pumps, scrub four times, rinse eight seconds, repeat until I feel better.

I can't believe this. It's fucking embarrassing. All I want to do is walk in front of a moving bus.

"Let us know when you are ready. Your mom and I will give you all the time you need." Dad walks over to join Mom on the bench. I'm surprised they are sitting so close to each other.

Pressure builds up in my chest like it's about to explode. Trying to stop something that makes me feel better is an impossible task, even if it doesn't make sense. How the heck am I supposed to control my body when it never lets up? Dr. Hannah said I have to choose to stop. I don't have a choice. Why the hell would I choose to be stuck in this prison?

## March 6

I never want to repeat yesterday again. I think I'm going to quit the team. I let everyone down and now the new coach thinks I'm crazy. Maybe I am. Maybe I've really sunk that low. The parents should take me in for a head scan. They must be so humiliated after yesterday.

-Daniel

## March 10

Dad's making me go to school today. He said he's going to drive me. Since I won't have my car, I can't leave school. I hope I don't lose it.

-Daniel

"Hello Daniel, have a seat." I walk into the school counselor's office, dreading the conversation that's about to take place. "We need to discuss the amount of school you are missing and the homework you are falling behind on."

"Yeah…" I plop in a chair and stare at her desk.

"I know you have a lot on your plate right now, but I also want to make sure you graduate on time."

"Me too."

"I have talked with your teachers and parents, and I have a thought for you. Don't get upset, just hear me out," Mrs. Lewis says.

Oh, this is going to be good.

"I think we need to consider other classroom options to help you focus and get your homework done on time. Smaller room, fewer students, more one-on-one help to keep you moving forward. I think going to Ms. Bender's classroom during the day would be very beneficial for you at this point."

"The special ed room?" I sit up and look her right in the eyes. "No way. No freaking way! I'm not stupid—I was supposed to be this year's valedictorian! There is no way I am going to sit in a class with a bunch of kids who don't remember their first name. You can't make me do that. No way in hell."

"That's a lot of judgmental assumptions. I understand why this would upset you, but listen for a moment. Right now the big goal here is to make sure you graduate on time, and with grades that are still desirable to most colleges. You do still want to go to college, don't you?"

Most colleges. A stone of regret drops into my stomach, to join all the other stones that fell in there this year. "Yes, I do."

"Then we need to explore our other options. We are trying to help you."

"By sticking me in a special ed classroom?" I can't even do school right.

"Daniel, like I said, that is not a very fair assessment of that classroom. You are over exaggerating it. This really isn't that big of a deal." She lets out a loud sigh and lays down her pen.

"Yeah, to you it isn't. But I'm the one still in high school. I'm the one who has to live with this label for the rest of my life. *Me.* Not *you.*"

"I tell you what. If you can prove to me and your teachers that you are going to try harder, and keep up with your schoolwork, and try your best not to miss any more school, then I will overlook this meeting and pretend it never happened. If you cannot do those things, then we will have to come back here and discuss this more seriously. Frankly, I am surprised by your reaction here today. This is not like you at all."

"I'm sorry. I'm not sure how I am supposed to feel about all of this." I grab my bag. "Can I go now?"

"Are you going to stay in the school building?"

"Yes," I lie. I am getting the hell out of here.

"Fine, I will talk to you tomorrow though."
"Bye."

## March 16

Mom and Dad are still upset about me skipping school again. Mom threatened to take off work and sit with me if I don't stop.

-Daniel

———

"Daniel? Are you in there?" Mr. Wilkerson walks over to my desk from the front of his classroom, speaking in hushed tones.

"What?" I startle and the room slowly comes back into focus.

"You were zoned out for a minute doing that finger thing you do when you are stressed out. Are you okay?"

"I'm sorry." I look back down at the Spanish test we were taking. Blank. Dammit.

"I don't think you will be able to finish that in ten more minutes... Why don't you go ahead and take it to Ms. Bender's classroom. She can proctor and give you more time to finish."

"What? No, I can finish it, I—"

"Daniel, it's all right, I am allowing you to have more time. If you stay here, you will have to turn it in when the timer goes off, regardless if you have finished it or not. Then I will have to give you whatever grade you get."

I notice other eyes turning in our direction. Kayla tries her best to keep her eyes on her test, but I can feel her sideways glance burning into my skull.

"Okay. I'll go." I grab my bag and stand up.

"Don't be ashamed Daniel, we just want to help you the best

we can." He speaks in a hushed tone as he guides me to the door and out into the hall. "I'll let Ms. Bender know you are on your way with your test."

"Thanks…" Crap. I can't believe this is happening. In front of everyone. I can't even finish a Spanish test. Why didn't I just start it? Why didn't I try to focus more? It's stupid that I get so anxious over this. I'm good at Spanish, why am I doing this?

One-two-three-four. Yes, I'll count my steps, that'll help me feel better. One-two, three, four. One, two, three, four—

"Hello, Daniel, hurry up so you can finish your test." Ms. Bender stands in the doorway of her classroom, waving her arm as if she was directing highway traffic.

"Uh, wait." I have to go back and re-count my steps. She interrupted me. One, two, three, four. One, two, three, four. One, two. Dammit, I'm at the door, I didn't finish. I need to go back. One, two, three, four—

"It's okay, I have all day. But you probably don't." She looks at her watch.

No, no, no, no. My steps aren't right. I have to get my steps right so I can focus on my test. If I don't get them right, I could fail, and I can't fail.

"*Daniel.* Please." The frown on her face could make a baby cry.

"I'm sorry. I'm coming." One, two, three, four. One, two, three, four. Better.

I walk into her classroom and am greeted by an array of bright, stimulating colors. Her room is painted in blues and yellows with a shag purple rug in the center of the room. The desks are arranged in a circle around the rug, with a large exercise ball in the center. Ten other kids sit around the circle.

A kid in a large wheelchair is in a corner with an assistant practicing the alphabet. It feels like I just walked into the twilight zone. I never knew this room existed.

"Have a seat right here please." She points to an empty desk right next to a kid I recognize from the soccer team doing math work. It catches me off guard. This kid doesn't have any problems, why is he here? "Come on, right here."

I have a seat and place my test on the desk. My pen fumbles to the floor. Shit. Shit. Shit. Shit.

"Are you going to pick it up?" She looks at me, obviously still trying to figure me out.

"No."

"Why not?"

"It's on the floor. If I pick it up, I'll have to go wash my hands."

"What if I pick it up for you?"

I shake my head.

"What if I pick it up and clean it with a Clorox wipe then hand it to you?"

"Uh... Can you do that?" Heat rises up in my face.

"I can definitely do that." Her sudden change in demeanor catches me off guard. She grabs a Clorox wipe from her desk and wipes off the pen. "Here is a fresh new pen. Mr. Wilkerson called and said you need to finish your Spanish test. Take your time. I'm here if you have any questions."

I give her a half-smile, take my pen and glance around the room one more time. The room is calmer than I expected.

Okay, I can do this.

I write my name at the top of my paper and start my Spanish test. I try not to think about where I am. I don't care where I am. My goal is to just finish high school. I need to graduate. I only have three months left. I can do this for three months, then I will never see most of these people again. Who cares that I'm sitting in a special ed class? It's just for three months. Then it's over. Right? This isn't a big deal. Is it?

"Daniel, you need to focus." Ms. Bender's voice brings me back to reality.

"Sorry." I start my test again. I can do this.

## March 25

I'm exhausted.

-Daniel

———

"All right, Daniel! It's good to see you. How was your week?" Dr. Hannah is chipper as ever.

"It was good." In fact, it wasn't very eventful.

"Did you miss any school this week?"

"Not too much." Two and a half days.

"Let's try to not miss any days this next week. You think you can do that?"

"I can try."

"Great! That is good to hear. Let's get started."

"Great." The more time he spends talking, the more time I have to stay in this room. This room where he obviously knocked a few books out of their place, folded up an end of the carpet and pushed the corner of the desk to make it crooked.

"If you're feeling up to it, I want to talk about your need for order and balance."

"...Okay?"

He flips through a couple of pages in his portfolio. "We haven't really talked about it yet, but this last fall when you were brought to the hospital, EMS wrote a few notes, and I noticed a few things when you were in observation about hitting or bumping your arms into walls or objects."

"Oh." My face heats up. It's really dumb. I know it doesn't make sense, but I can't always help it.

"Is this something you want to talk about?"

I shrug.

"We can stop any time."

I nod.

"Do you remember when you had to be brought into the hospital?"

I cringe at the memory but nod again.

"What was your thought process when you were hitting your arms on the wall?"

I shrug.

He nods and writes down a few notes. I can only look at my hands. We sit in silence for a few moments. Maybe he thinks I'm trying to come up with a good answer.

"If you say it out loud, I can help figure out what to do if you ever find yourself in that situation again. Only if you are ready, though. From personal experience, the more you shine a light on what's going on inside that head of yours, the more we can help stop all those bad thoughts in their tracks."

I know he's right. But how do I put this into words? How do I explain the feeling of being unbalanced and the urgent need to fix it? I try to organize my thoughts. "If I'm unbalanced, I can't concentrate. If I can't concentrate, then everything becomes unorganized in my head, and if everything becomes unorganized, I disappoint everyone around me because I can't do anything right." I slouch in my chair and tap my fingers on my sternum.

"Hmm." He writes something down. "You cannot stop a thought from popping into your head, no one can. Just like you can't control random feelings or sensations that pop up in your body. That's not your fault. It's something that happens to all of us. But when you have OCD, it happens in excess and on repeat. What you *can* do is this: Imagine a stop sign, or a brick wall. Whenever those strings of thoughts or feelings pop into your head, throw that wall in front of them! Or, better yet, yell STOP! Really loud."

"Yeah, because that won't cause a scene." I think I've already embarrassed myself enough this year.

"I am dead serious. You have to stop that thought in its tracks and ignore it. Don't act on it if you can help it, don't look at it. Turn around and shut your eyes. Do whatever you have to do so you are not dwelling on it."

"But how?"

"Acknowledge the feeling. It's there, it exists. However, the next step is that you have to acknowledge that not all of our feelings are truthful or helpful. The same with your thoughts that get stuck in a loop. Or your need to wash your hands. You can say, 'I see you, I feel you, but this isn't your home, and you need to leave now.' If that's unbearable, allow yourself to wash your hands once. Because really, that's all you need to help make the germs go away. If your body is screaming for balance too loudly, go ahead and tap both sides. Just once. But remember you are in ultimate control of your body. Do you think you can try that?"

"I can try, but it seems impossible."

"Difficult, yes. But impossible? No. OCD is an anxiety disorder. And sometimes with anxiety we have to power through until our brains realize that something isn't that bad. Or until your brain realizes that it's in control. And in your case, you're on medication to help with that. Because let's be honest, our brains need a little help from time to time. Or a lot of help. How about this: next time you're afraid of getting stuck in a loop, you can call or text me right away. Deal?"

"Sure."

"Let's do a little role-play." Dr. Hannah stands up. "You stand up too."

Oh geez. My heart jumps a little, but I stand up anyway.

"Okay, close your eyes, and I'm going to pick a random age, and you're going to tell me what your biggest worry at that age was and why."

"Why?" I shift back and forth on my feet. "And why does this require standing?"

"Sometimes it helps to get up and to get the blood flowing a bit, to move around if you want to. As for your previous why, sometimes with anxiety, there is a trigger. Something that happened to you or around you that caused it all to begin. And if that's the case, it would be helpful to identify that trigger so you can understand it more."

My heart speeds up. This doesn't sound very enjoyable.

"Ready?" Dr. Hannah does a quick jog in place and shakes out his arms.

I nod.

"All right. Close your eyes. You are thirteen. What is the biggest thing you are worried about? What gives you the most anxiety?"

I close my eyes, then open them to see if he was watching. His eyes are closed too, so I quickly close mine again. "Thirteen?" I repeat. "Probably making the soccer team that year. I was in a new league and most of the kids were bigger than me. Even some of the girls. It was a co-ed league."

"Did you make the team?"

I nod, then quickly remember our eyes are closed. "Yeah. It was a really good year. I had a lot of fun."

"M-kay. Now you're nine. What is nine-year-old Daniel most worried about?"

"New school. New friends. New town. My parents got married that summer and we moved closer to where Dad's job was."

"That's a pretty big transition. Why did those things bother you?"

"I was afraid that Dad was going to decide he didn't like us and I would be all alone again."

"What else?"

"That I wouldn't make any friends because I was weird."

"And what really happened? What's the truth?"

"Dad didn't leave and I met my best friend. It ended up being an okay year. I had some struggles with OCD, the whole balance thing and anxiety, but I had Garrett, and nobody liked him at the time... so we were inseparable from the start."

"Okay, I'm going to go back a few more years."

"Okay." I know where this is going, and I'm not sure if I'm prepared for it or not.

"You're five years old. What is your biggest worry?"

A dagger slams into my heart. I hate thinking about anything that happened before life with Dad.

"Take your time." Dr. Hannah breathes out.

"F-five. Um. My biggest worry? That I was going to be forgotten about. Abandoned."

"Those are some huge worries for a five-year-old. Why did you feel that way?"

"Mom had so many boyfriends. Always in and out. I always

thought they would stay, but they never stayed. And I was forgotten about. Mom left me alone for hours, and I had to feed myself sometimes. Sometimes her boyfriends would yell at her. Or me. They always left. Mom would always end up crying over it, and I would always feel guilty because I could never make her feel better."

"It wasn't your job to make her feel better. You were just five."

I sigh and open my eyes to find my chair and plop back down. "I guess. But she was all I had then. It was never enough. I was never enough for them. I was never enough for her…"

"Was it your job to be enough for her?"

"I don't know. Maybe." A tear sneaks up on me.

"The answer is no. You were five. Even now, the answer is no. You're only seventeen."

"Almost eighteen."

"It's still no. You had a really stressful life at a very young age. You put so much pressure on such a little guy. So did your mom. No parent is perfect, all parents make mistakes. And sometimes those mistakes really affect us in deep unexplainable ways. And that can come out in depression, or anxiety. They can be coping mechanisms for things we cannot explain. Childhood trauma really messes with your brain chemistry."

"Trauma." I huff out. "She never laid a hand on me."

"Maybe that is part of the issue. Neglect and abandonment can be just as debilitating as physical and verbal abuse."

That takes my breath away and leaves my lungs burning. Is what happened so long ago why I was so terrified of Dad leaving and forgetting about me? Is that why I don't really feel so close to Mom?

"That's a lot to process, isn't it?"

I nod. My body feels numb.

"What are your thoughts on that?"

I shrug. My body weighs a thousand pounds. "I don't know. I really need to go home and take a nap now."

Dr. Hannah nods. "Yeah. I feel that. This was a lot of heavy today. If you go home and your thoughts throw you into your compulsions, I am serious about saying 'stop' out loud. It is pretty effective. And you'll be needing to remind yourself that sometimes feelings are just feelings, and feelings are not always accurate. That's why it's important to stop them in their tracks."

"I'll try it." I hope it works.

"Please call me anytime. Even if it's after dark. See you next week, Daniel." Dr. Hannah gets up and opens the door for me like he does after every meeting. I walk out the door and walk right past the knocked over books on the shelves.

## March 26

I still can't stop thinking about yesterday's session with Dr. Hannah. I feel sick to my stomach that I said that stuff about my mom out loud. I've never told anyone that, maybe because I was still in denial to myself over it.

I used to get so upset when she would come home every other weekend with a new boyfriend who promised to be my dad. They would leave me in the living room with a movie and a TV dinner and go lock themselves in her room and not come out for hours, or even all night. I remember having to put myself to bed as a kindergartner.

Then he came. My dad, the one guy who could see through all her defenses. He dug past her garbage and swept her away. He had a good job, came from a good family, and he was decisive and knew what he wanted.

When they were dating, I would get on my knees by my bed and pray that he would stay. I prayed that he would love me enough to stay, even with all of mom's garbage. I promised myself that I would be good and obedient. I had convinced myself that's why he stayed—because I tried my best to be the perfect son. I always got good grades and I hardly ever got into trouble.

He made enough money to keep Mom content and free to do whatever she wanted, and he was kind enough to want to spend time with *me* and get to know me. I had never had that before.

When we moved at the beginning of fourth grade, I never told anyone he was my stepdad. I never talked about life before him. Life when Mom was on the verge of being a hooker, and I had to learn to cook for myself by the time I was five. Why would I? I didn't want anyone to think that I was trash. I had a new image to uphold. I was the son of a podiatrist, and I decided to call Mom an artist long ago. She likes to paint. Sometimes she would sell her stuff. With Dad making enough money, she had more time to paint and do what she wanted.

Now everything's ruined. My life isn't going to be the same. I have no idea what Mom is thinking, and I wish I knew so I could fix it.

I don't know what I'm trying to say. It's late, and now I am rambling. In my journal. Where no one will see the shit that I'm going through. It's better this way. I think.

-Daniel

## April 1

I think if you have OCD, it would only be fair if you had a restart button. That way if you accidentally spend two hours in the morning giving into a compulsion of, say, washing your hands or rearranging your books so you would feel better, you could hit said button and go back in time. This way you wouldn't be late for school, like I am this morning. Again.

-Daniel

———

"How do you think you did on that calculus quiz?" Garrett asks me as he opens his locker to throw his books in.

"I don't know. I almost didn't finish, I got stuck trying to rearrange the problems. At this point, I'm pretty sure the teacher won't even be able to read my work." I stare at the floor to watch where I am standing, trying not to think of my raw burning hands. Maybe I should get a different soap for home.

"Sucks man. I'm sure you fucking aced it. Calculus was one of your best subjects."

"They were all my best subjects at one point." When did I become such a loser?

"Don't stress." Garrett shrugs. "But speaking of stress..." He pulls a breath into his cheeks before making a fart noise. "You haven't been at soccer practice for a while..."

Shit. "Yeah, sorry. I just have a lot on my plate right now. You know?"

Garrett nods... in agreement? Just to make me feel better? "I talked to the coach, and the team, and they are all okay with you showing up randomly. Even to just join us for practice. Fuck man, I know you have a lot of shit going on right now… but don't drop out on everything…"

I loop my hand through my backpack strap and tap my thumb on my sternum in beats of four. I don't want to drop everything. It's not something I'm consciously doing. All my energy is going to trying to think straight. Everything else seems so gray and empty. But I don't know how to explain that to anyone. The once predicted valedictorian, captain of the soccer team, reduced to what? A frightened child who has breakdowns in the middle of Spanish class.

"Have you decided if you're going to prom yet?"

I shake my head. "Did you ask Sara?"

"Oh yeah, a while ago. I thought I told you already." He grins. "You should go."

"Nope. It's too stressful to think about."

"I'll be there to hold your hand if you want." He grins and wiggles his eyebrows.

"Scandal. What would Sara think?" I attempt a grin back.

"Oh, I'm sure she'd understand. There is a time to party, and a time to take care of our children."

"Shut up." I find that statement both amusing and humiliating.

"I'm sure if you show up, you'll get some rando to dance with you so Sara and I can have our adult time." He puts his arms up like he's dancing and spins around in a circle. "Think about it."

The thought of some random person holding my hands makes me feel gross. "Hey, I'll meet you in the library in a few."

"Gotta wash your hands?" He crosses his arms across his chest.

"Uh, why do you care?" That's a stupid question.

"Your dad called me. Asked me to be your brick wall. Like when we were kids and those assholes were picking on you."

"Seriously?"

"Yeah, I thought it was a bit too bromance-y, but, fuck it. I'm your brick wall." An asinine smile spreads across his face.

Is this really happening?

"Self-control, Daniel, self-control. You can do that finger thingy if it helps." He points to my already tapping thumb. "I won't judge. Not anymore that is."

"Fine." I let out a huff and push past him to get to the library. If I was an engine, I'm sure you would see steam fuming out of my ears.

"Hey, careful. You can't just bulldoze past a brick wall like that," he shouts behind me. "I'm a fucking brick wall baby! Now get back here—"

"Shut up." This is my life now.

Garrett lets out a deep belly laugh.

## April 5

I know the team says I can come back, but I'm done. I'm done with soccer. I can't do it, I can't take the pressure. I hate myself for it. Soccer was my life. A scout promised that he was going to come watch me this season. I've thrown it all away. My whole future.

No more scholarships, nothing. I don't even know if I will make it to college. My GPA has dropped to the point where none of the other schools will look at me. Sure, I could pull the disability card if I wanted to, but I can't. I won't do that.

If I want any kind of future, I need to start applying to some state schools. Huge, enormous state universities with a billion people. So many people. My heart is racing just thinking about it.

Shit. Shit. Shit. Shit. It doesn't help me feel better writing that down four times.

-Daniel

"Dude, you should have been at the last game. It was fucking amazing!" Garrett throws himself across my bed. I pretend to ignore the pillows that fall on the floor.

"Yeah? Sorry I missed it." Not really. Avoiding huge crowds of people seems to be my thing these days.

"Sure you are, asshole." He picks up a pillow and throws it at my face. A pillow that was on the floor. I immediately walk into my bathroom and start washing my hands without even thinking about it.

"Come on, Daniel. I haven't even been here for five minutes and you're already starting that."

He's right. "Stop." Turn off the damn water.

"What did I do?"

"Oh, not you. Sorry, forget it." I walk over to my desk and sit down in the rolling chair, and slowly wheel myself towards Garrett. "So, hey, I have something I want to tell you. I'm not sure how you'll take it, because I've never told anyone before, and I'm afraid you'll get pissed that I've been lying to you since the fourth grade."

"What the fuck? You're a penguin! I knew it!" He throws his hands up in the air.

"Shut up, dude. I'm trying to be serious."

"You're always trying to be serious."

I stare at him.

"Fine, continue, Daniel," he says sarcastically and gestures his hand in the air.

"Um, yeah." I rub my hand across my face. Why is this so hard? What difference is it going to make anyway? Could he really get mad over this? Why didn't I just tell him forever ago?

"Jeez, is everything okay? You seem nervous." He sits up on the bed.

"You know my dad?"

"Yeah."

"He's really my stepdad. He and my mom got married when I was in third grade. Right before we moved here, when I met you in grade school."

"Whoa. Okay."

He looks confused. He is confused. What do I say now?

"Where's the sperm donor?"

"I don't know. One-night stand probably." My face heats up at record speeds.

"Shit. Man, why didn't you ever tell me?"

"Are you pissed?" Please say no, tell me it's fine.

"Wow. Am I pissed? That's what you're worried about right now?" He sighs. "I don't know. On one hand, no. I get it, leave the past in the past to avoid all those old feelings. Yeah, I understand that. On the other hand, I'm your best fucking friend. Why didn't you ever tell me?"

"I know—"

"No, I don't think you do. You've known me for a long time. We used to go on camping trips, sleepovers. Heck, I fucking lived with you, remember? When my dad was hitting me before my parents divorced?"

"Garrett—"

"Just, let me finish, okay?"

"Sorry." I look down at my hands. I feel disgusting, like a filthy child covered in sticky drool and mud from playing outside with a sucker in their mouth. My skin feels thick and dry between my fingers. I know the only thing that will quench the hot desert sand on my skin is to take a shower.

"You don't get to say sorry yet. You saw all this shit happening to me, and you still let me believe you had the perfect life. That nothing bad ever happened to you. You were the perfect kid, you never got in trouble, your dad never hit you. You don't think sharing any of that with me could have helped me? You never once thought that telling me this bit of information would have changed my outlook on the world? Knowing that fucking shit can happen to anyone? You're a fucking asshole Daniel, you know that?" He drops his heavy head on his propped-up arm resting on his knee.

I don't know what to say. He's right. I'm a fucking asshole. Another stone drops into my stomach. I've disappointed him too.

"Shit. A fucking one-night stand." He crosses his arms across his chest and waits for me to speak. "Now you can apologize."

I bite the insides of my cheeks. I hate hearing that out loud. "Me not telling you was selfish. I had made up my mind that I wasn't going to tell anyone before we even met. After a while I just forgot, I blocked it out. It felt like my stepdad was my dad forever. He adopted me right away, and he never once told anyone that I was his stepson. He used to say the word 'step' was a cheap cop-out." I sigh. I screwed up, but I didn't mean to. "Look, I'm telling you now. I'm sorry, man, I don't know what else to say."

"Dude, you're more screwed up than I thought." Garrett breathes out.

"Yeah?"

"Yeah. You're a fucking bastard. My parents were at least married when they had me." He laughs. "I mean, I know my fucking dad. I wish I didn't most days. So maybe you're kind of lucky in a way. Bastard."

"Feel better now?" Go ahead and laugh. Asshole.

"No, not yet." He stands up and holds out his hand with a dumbass smile across his face. "Don't lie to me again you bastard."

"Will you stop calling me a bastard?"

"Only if I can say it one more time."

"Deal."

"You fucking bastard." Yup, that dumbass smile is still there.

I grab his hand and we do our secret handshake we used to do in elementary school. When he drops my hand, my first instinct is to get up and go to the sink to wash my hands.

"Brick wall baby. Fucking brick wall." He steps in front of me.

"I hate you, you know that?"

"Yeah, I can live with hate, knowing that you are illegitimate and I am not."

"Dumbass."

We burst out in laughter. It feels good. It's been a long time since I have laughed like this.

## April 8

Dad moved out today. I knew it was coming, but I thought he would try to stay until graduation like he said he would. I tried preparing myself the best I could, but I still can't breathe. My heart is caught up in my throat and I want to cry. All I want to do is cry like a little kid, but I can't. That well is dried up.

I stood in the shower for over an hour this morning, which made me late for school, which made me not want to go to school. My skin was so raw from the scrubbing, it hurt to put clothes on anyway.

Who's going to help me now that he's gone? Mom's kind of shut down. It reminds me of when I was little, before she met Dad. Why does this have to happen before graduation? Why isn't she the one leaving? I still feel like it's my fault, even though I know it's not. I don't like feeling like I am disgusting still, but I can't get clean no matter how many times I try to wash my body.

I need to see Dr. Hannah again, but I'm not sure I can wait until tomorrow. I might call him. Would that be stupid? He's probably used to stuff like this right? Of course he is.

-Daniel

"Hello?"
"Dr. Hannah?"
"Yes?"
"Uh, it's Daniel."

"Why hey there, Daniel! Shouldn't you be in school right now?"

"Yeah, probably."

"What can I do for you?"

I hold my breath. I didn't think I would cry about this. Ever.

"Daniel?"

"M-my dad moved out today."

"Oh, wow. I'm sorry buddy. That's really hard." His sigh blows through the receiver and into my ear.

"I-I can't take it, I can't stop scrubbing my body. I know it's stupid, it doesn't make sense. It makes me feel better for a moment, but then it goes away so I have to do it again."

"Have you been taking your pills?"

"Yes, every day. I even took anxiety stuff today, but I can't stop. I can't stop, I want to stop, but I can't-can't, can't. STOP. Dammit. C-can I come in now?" I push away a tear.

"You know what, I have lunch in forty-three minutes. How about you come in then? Do you think you can stay out of the shower until then?"

"I don't know," I snap. "Maybe. Yes, of course I can." Why am I angry at him?

"All right, I will see you in forty-three minutes."

"Thanks."

"Do you need me to call your mom and tell her?"

"No. I'll tell her," I lie.

Okay, I can wait forty-three minutes. Forty-three minutes? Who the hell says forty-three minutes? Why didn't he just round up? He did that on purpose. Forty-three instead of forty-five, or just forty. He had to say forty-three. Jerk. I'm an idiot.

"Come on in. I hope you don't mind me eating my sandwich."

I shake my head as he takes an enormous bite out of his sandwich while sitting at the desk.

"Have a seat, friend. How's it going?"

My hands shake as I shove them deeper into my pockets. "Are you sure it's okay for me to be here right now?"

"Of course! That's what I'm here for, and if I'm available, I want to help."

"My dad moved out today."

"I know. I am really sorry." Dr. Hannah puts his sandwich down and comes over to where I am sitting. "That's really rough, buddy." His eyes move to the abrasions covering my arms and neck. "Daniel, what's that you have on your skin?"

I quickly take my hands out of my pockets and try to cover my arms with them. "Nothing. I just scrubbed too hard. I'm fine." I'm not fine. I still feel disgusting.

"Do you mind if I look at your arms? Does it look like this anywhere else?"

"Uh." The stinging across my chest screams out, begging to be helped. "Not really." I hold out my arm for him to look at.

"Is this from scrubbing too?" He points to my jaw.

Dammit. Why did I even come here? I nod my head.

"Daniel, I'm afraid I'm going to have to call your parents. I am going to call the ward and see if they have any open beds."

"No, I'm okay, really I am. I just had a weak moment, I can do better—"

"I know you don't mean to, but you are still unintentionally harming yourself."

"I can't go back to the hospital." The vein on the top of my head starts buzzing as my face glows from the heat.

"Daniel, I can't in good conscience let you leave here today after something like this because I am afraid of what you might do if you go home. I thought we were getting better, buddy, and I want to make sure you are all right. I'll be right back, I'm going to call your mom and the hospital to see if they have a bed open for you."

He leaves the room and I wipe away a wayward tear that escapes. I can't go back to the hospital. I can't go back there. Shit. Shit. Shit. Shit. I sit in silence for what seems like forever until Dr. Hannah returns. The silence is almost deafening.

"Your mom is on her way, and you're in luck! They have a spot for you." He sits across from me. "She is also rather upset, she thought you were at school. You didn't tell her you were here?"

"I, uh, must have forgotten to call her."

He cocks his head to the side and gives me an odd look.

"Look, Dr. Hannah, I'm fine. I feel better already—it's just a rough day. Am I not entitled to having one of those occasionally?"

"Of course you are. We all are entitled to bad days, or even a bad week, maybe a bad month depending on what life throws at you. But most of us who have a bad day don't spend hours in the shower scrubbing off our skin when they can't cope with whatever life has thrown at them. We usually call a friend, cry for a bit, or eat a chocolate bar. What you did is not a normal reaction. You need to understand that." He sighs. "How are you feeling right now?"

I feel like crying like a baby. I feel like dumping scalding water over my skin so I can get rid of all these nasty spirals. I feel like digging a hole and living in it. I feel like shaking the hell out of my mother and demanding her to give me answers. I feel like screaming at my dad at the top of my lungs, asking him why he didn't fight harder. I feel like not existing so I don't feel like a freak anymore. I feel... "I'm fine."

Mom walks in through the door. "Daniel! What is going on? Are you okay? Oh honey, I'm so sorry—" She rushes over to give me a hug over my limp arms.

Shards of glass scrape over my body. I try not to breathe.

"I'm sorry about all of this, Mrs. Quincy. I was under the impression that Daniel had called you."

"It's okay, as long as he's safe, that's all that matters." She reaches over and brushes the hair out of my face.

Why does she keep touching me? She knows I don't like being touched. She knows how hard it is for me to have her hanging over me. I can't handle it.

"Well, take him on over to the fourth-floor psych wing at the hospital. Dr. West is expecting him."

I stand up quickly to break the hold my mom has around my chest.

"Thank you, Dr. Hannah. Thank you for everything. Come on Daniel." Mom shakes his hand and pushes me out the door.

I can't even look Dr. Hannah in the eyes. Mostly because I feel like the stupid one. Maybe I'm embarrassed, but I can't tell, all I feel is numb. I can't go back to the hospital, everyone will find out and know I can't handle living like a normal person. I just want to be normal. Why is it fair that I have to deal with this shit?

"I'll come check on you tomorrow, Daniel." Dr. Hannah's voice is apologetic. It doesn't help me feel better.

## April 10

48 hours of my life on hold.

48 hours of he can't be alone.

48 hours of feeling like a freak.

48 hours of my mom crying over me.

48 hours of therapists and doctors.

48 hours of not being able to sleep.

48 hours of being stuck in a hospital.

48 hours of not being allowed to shower.

48 hours of my dignity going down the drain.

48 hours of being treated as a self-harm case.

48 hours of Mom begging me not to hurt myself.

48 hours of being unable to talk to my best friend.

48 hours of dad repeating to me that it's not my fault.

48 hours of the parents fighting about whose fault this is.

48 hours of stinging pain after nurses re-cleaned my abrasions.

48 hours of dictators spelling the amount of hand washing I can do.

48 hours of the same questions over and over again from doctors and nurses.

48 hours of holding back a dam of anger and tears that threatened to bring me down.

48 hours of me being asked to take my shirt off so they could see all that I did to myself.

48 hours of Mom on the phone telling her friends she's afraid her son is going to commit suicide.

-Daniel

"Hey." Garrett walks through the kitchen door and plops himself right next to me at the kitchen counter.

"Are you hungry?" Mom asks as she places her freshly made sandwich right in front of him.

"Yes please!" He grabs the sandwich and takes a huge bite.

"Hey to you too." I clear my throat and lean farther onto the counter.

"Hey," he says again around another bite of food.

I wait until he's done eating as Mom pushes my sandwich closer to me. I push it towards Garrett instead. I still don't have much of an appetite.

"I know you just got back from the hospital again." He takes another huge bite. "But the soccer guys are kind of getting together after prom, and we all really want you to be there."

"I'm not going to prom—"

"That's right, he's not," Mom cuts in. "It's not a good idea." She gives me an apologetic glance and makes herself another sandwich.

"Whoa, hear me out." He puts the sandwich down and folds his hands in front of him. "The team is putting together something really special, and it would really suck balls if Daniel couldn't be there."

"Ah. Suck balls, huh?" Mom taps the counter and looks at me before giving her attention back to Garrett. "I don't know. I don't think it's a good idea for Daniel to go anywhere right now."

I'm torn. It would be amazing to feel like I don't have any problems for a night. But at the same time, I'm exhausted and anxious. I shrug and look at Garrett, waiting for his rebuttal.

"Look, I know you're nervous about Daniel, and I get it, a lot of us are. But we graduate soon, you know? And I'll be there! I'll keep an eye on Daniel the whole time. We won't even stay out too late. Please?" He slaps on the widest smile in his arsenal.

She sighs as I wait for her comeback. She surprises me and asks, "What do you want?"

"Oh. Uh…" I pull in a deep breath and try to weigh out the pros and cons.

"If you have a freak-out, we can come back here, no questions asked. But you should really go," Garrett begs.

Mom nods.

"Yeah?" That takes out some of the anxiety. "Maybe I should stop by, even to just say hi?"

Mom nods again.

"Really?"

"I'm nervous about it. Is it just the soccer team?" she asks Garrett.

"Yeah, just the team. No alcohol."

"Okay."

I smile as excitement floods my body for a moment, followed by mixed emotions. I'll be fine. Garrett will be there. I know these guys.

"Fuck yes! I mean, thank you!" Garrett picks up my uneaten sandwich. "I gotta go. I'll text you, Daniel! Bye!" With that he sprints out of the house.

"Do you want me to make you another sandwich?" Mom picks up the empty plate.

"No, I'm fine. Thanks." A smile threatens to break free on my face. "I'm going to go catch up on homework."

## April 14

He's late. The one time I loan him my car, he's late. Never again. What if he got in an accident? What if he's hurt and laying on the side of the road? What if Sara freaked out and slit his throat? That sounds more likely than him wrecking my car.

-Daniel

———

I take in a deep breath and pound my chest four times until I spot a set of lights pull into the driveway. I run down the stairs and out the front door, slamming the door a little too hard. I wince at the sound. I hope I didn't wake Mom up...

"Hey, thanks for letting me borrow your car. I'm sorry I'm so late. We ended up talking for a while over ice cream." Garrett tosses me my keys and gets into the passenger side.

"Yeah? Are you madly in love with this girl now?" I hold the keys in my hand. Did he keep them in his pocket? He probably set them on a table... I get into the driver side and start the engine, then rub my hand on my jeans. Not that it helps.

"Fuck no, man! She's sweet. I probably made her glow bright red about twenty times. I think that's a new record for me."

"Really?" I back into the street and head down the road.

Garrett smiles at me. "Who knows what the future may bring. Sara has a lot of shit to work through, and I really hope she makes it out to the other side. I've been where she is."

It's a mix of strange and refreshing at the same time to see Garrett open up like he has been lately.

"You can't fix everybody you meet, you know."

"No, but what good am I if I don't try? Look at you, for example. You can't live without your brick wall. You're welcome."

I roll my eyes. "We're late to the party, I'm not sure who all's going to still be there." I huff out some of my frustration.

"I know, man. I'm really sorry."

"It's not that big of a deal. Maybe I'm a little jealous of you having all the fun." I smile at him. "Did you kiss her?"

"Why would I share such sacred and precious information? Why would a germaphobe want to hear the details of me swapping spit with another human being?"

"So you didn't kiss her?"

"Nope. She gives great hugs though."

"Oh, friend-zoned." I laugh.

"There was so much friend-zoning going on."

"Ha, sorry."

"Fuck that, man, this fall we will be around college girls! I can't be seen with a high schooler."

"Good call." There's the Garrett I know.

He turns up the radio and rolls down his window. "I can't believe we are graduating next month. I feel like my life is finally starting! I can finally be free of my deadbeat parents and sleep in a bed without—"

Bright lights disappear into the sound of crushing metal, lifting the car into the air. I'm weightless as glass flies past my face. My body hits a giant white deceivingly hard cloud of fabric, popping my neck back. The back of my head slams into the headrest. Screaming metal and sparks surround me. My arms fly up over my head like I'm stuck on a roller coaster from hell as we flip head over tail across the road. The ground finally catches the roof, not once, but twice as we roll-skid to a stop.

I'm dead. Oh shit. My lungs burn with every careful inhale. I don't know what's broken. I don't know if I can even move. Dust continues to blow in through the busted windshield and blinds me.

Shit. I'm upside down. I can't move. God, I can't move! I suck in another deep breath, coughing out the dust that settles into my nostrils.

I wiggle my fingers and feel up and down my middle. Every inch of my body is screaming.

I'm okay. I think I'm okay.

"Garrett? Are you all right?" I carefully turn my head to a severed seat belt and an empty passenger seat. My heart stops. "Shit!" Fumbling for my buckle, I slide the short distance to the crushed roof and crawl out where the windshield once was. I'm forced to pause with my hands and knees digging into the grass as everything around me spins.

One-two-three-four-Fuck. Stop. Find Garrett! I stand up too quickly and my knees buckle, bringing me back towards the embankment. Looking at my hands, I notice about a dozen little cuts on my palms. My breath catches in my throat as I rub my hands on my jeans. A thousand fire ants crawl through my bloodstream as I push back the tears.

Not now... Focus! I stand up again, this time more slowly and search the scene for Garrett.

Four teenagers climb out of a bright yellow SUV, still in prom gear, crying and clinging to each other.

"Garrett! Where are you?" I run to the back of the car, frantically searching for my friend.

"Uh..."

I run over to the moan coming from behind the tree. "Garrett! How the hell did you end up over here!?"

"I-uh, I can f-fly." A puddle of blood surrounds his body.

"You're bleeding—"

"Y-you're bleeding."

I look down at my hands again, then at the open wound on his chest, the source of the puddle. One-two-three-four-one-two-three-four. My vision is blurred by too many tears. Tears that I wish would turn into rain, to clean off my body, to clean my hands. I take a step back from Garrett. I can't touch him. I fucking can't touch him. My body screams at me again, begging me to bring back its balance. I squeeze my eyes shut, hoping the pressure would help calm the rest of my insides down.

"D-daniel, M-my chest h-hurts... A-am I okay?" He takes in a shaky breath as blood continues to flow down his chest, a crimson river of life, soaking into the grass.

"You're going to be fine, Garrett. Okay? Can you hear the sirens? That could be an ambulance."

Silence follows. Shit shit shit shit. I pound my chest with my fist as hard as I can, tears mingle with the blood on my shirt.

"FUCK!" I grab my throbbing head and take a step closer to Garrett. What the hell is wrong with me? Just go to him!

The yellow SUV speeds past me and down the road. "What the hell are you doing? Get the fuck back here!!" Shit. Get a grip, Daniel!

I rush over to Garrett and stand over his limp body. That first aid class last year was no help for the panic. I know I need to stop the bleeding, but I have cuts on my hands. I can't. Shit. I yank off my button-up shirt and wad it into a ball. I take a step closer and slip in the grass that is now covered in his blood, covering my arms and undershirt in red. One-two-three-four-one-two-three-four.

Are you just going to let him die? Are you going to let Garrett die?! I push my shirt into the river coming out of his chest and put my whole body weight on top of him.

"I'm so sorry, Garrett, please don't die. God, I'm so sorry!" The minutes feel like hours. The whooshing sound in my ears is so loud, I can't tell if the sirens are getting closer or farther away.

Did he stop breathing? I look at his eyes "Garrett! No!"

In a rush of fear and clarity, I stuff my shirt further into the wound and lean over his chest with both hands over his heart to try and stop the bleeding.

One, two, three, four. One two three four. I lean down to listen for a heartbeat. I can't hear it over my pounding head. One two three four. One two three four. I keep leaning on his chest, desperate. One two three four. I don't try to listen anymore, because I can't think.

My skin prickles up and my heart speeds up, pounding into my bones. All I want to do is run away from all of this.

One. Two. Three. Four. One. Two. Three. Four. One. Two. Three. Four.

"Son? You can let go now, help is here." A larger than life police officer towers over me, even with his hands on top of mine. Blue and red lights flash in my eyes.

"N-no, I can't let go—"

"It's all right, we will take care of him."

"Is he going to be okay? The SUV came out of nowhere-then they just left-and I couldn't touch him, but he stopped talking-and—"

"It's ok, he's still breathing," the EMT interrupts "We've got him now."

"Come on, let them take care of your friend." The police officer pulls me away as an EMS crew scrambles towards Garrett and puts him on a gurney.

The flashing lights blind me as I turn around.

"Son, is that your blood? Are you hurt?" The officer's voice raises a few decibels.

"What? Oh... no, it's his..."

"Who was driving?" His voice gets serious.

"Uh, I-I was. Is he going to be okay?"

"Were you drinking?"

"No..."

"We just busted a party down the road for underage drinking."

"I-I wasn't... It was the SUV."

"Can you give me a description?"

"Uh..." Was it yellow? White? "Yellow. I think."

My knees go weak and I fall back into the grass, my face in my bloody hands. Giant sobs wreck my body, as the pain of the shards of glass throb on the top of my head. My body disconnects from my mind as I give in to the gravity, and the darkness pulling me down.

## April 15

I don't know how to start. It's almost sickly hilarious how quickly life can change. In less than a second. Is it our body that carries life? Or our souls, floating through the atmosphere, brushing our loved ones' cheeks with our fingertips, desperately trying to make sure they don't forget us?

I hate thinking about death. I remember when Garrett's little sister died when we were in tenth grade. I didn't know her that well, but the way Garrett carried around an overwhelming amount of sadness for what seemed like forever, it made me feel like I knew her. Until one day he shoved that sadness so far inside of his soul, there was nothing left but a bitter glow that hung out around his eyes. He just decided to stop talking about her one day.

I asked him about it once, and he said it's because people stopped talking about her, and feeling like he was the only one keeping her alive was too painful. That no one else deserved to hear about her, so he kept her to himself.

Grief has always been one of those topics I've tried to avoid. I've dealt with it in different kinds of ways when I was little. Like every time I thought I had a new dad, but then the next week he would disappear. But grief caused by death? I've never had to deal with that before.

Garrett's headed into his third surgery this afternoon. The doctors have nothing to say one way or another. Just if we're the praying type, pray.

Mom's been at the hospital with his mom since last night. She regained her sanity once she realized I made it out with a mild concussion and five stitches on my forehead.

Dad stayed the night here at the house last night, and will for a few nights. It's been nice, but weird at the same time. He keeps following me around, making sure I'm okay, talking me through panic attacks from the car accident... and keeping me from scrubbing the stitches right out of my head...

I don't know what I will do if Garrett doesn't make it. I can't do this without my best friend.

-Daniel

## April 16

I got stuck in my morning ritual this morning. Dad came early to take me to school and got a bit frustrated. He nearly pushed me out the front door this morning so I wouldn't be late. He apologized. It's dumb, I know, but I just want Garrett to be safe.

He hasn't woken up yet. Mom said they're just going to let him wake up on his own, but that everything went well. He still has all of his limbs and fingers. I can go see him the moment he's out of ICU. He's predicted to have a fast recovery, according to the doctors, because he's young and healthy. I'll believe it when I can actually see him.

At school today, a bunch of the soccer team got into a fight with those kids who had been drinking at prom. I was in the school library catching up on homework, and I could hear it down the hall. All the yelling made my heart jump into my throat. The librarian closed the double doors into the library and called the front office to see what was going on. I'm glad to be home now.

-Daniel

Dad lets out a huff and sits down on the opposite side of the couch from me. "Got some news…" He breathes out.

No. I can feel the blood draining from my face. "Is it Garrett? Is he okay-is he—"

"Stop." He closes the distance between us and places both of his hands firmly on my shoulders. "It's not about Garrett—"

"Then what?"

"Calm down, I'm getting there." He drops his hands and folds them in his lap. "The police caught the drunk driver. There were a couple witnesses at the scene, and a few of the kids in the SUV with him confessed."

"Kids?"

"Well, teens. From your school. Did you know Dean Wight?"

I shake my head, my palms sweating, feeling thick and dirty.

"He's a senior at your school. Just turned eighteen a few months ago."

Goosebumps prick up all over my body. His name is familiar, but I don't think I've ever met him. And now his life is screwed up before it really started. "What's going to happen to him?"

Dad shrugs. "A DUI for sure. The rest will depend on the judge and if Garrett's mother wants to fight."

"Garrett would never let her." Garrett would go up to Dean and give him a hug, probably tell him not to worry about it, just to get his shit together and never do it again.

Dad lets out another sigh and rubs his face. "I'm glad you're okay. I have no idea what I would do without you around."

I lean in for a hug, my racing heart finally slows down to a human level of pumping. I'm thankful to be alive, even when my mind goes to shit and I lose control. I'm thankful that it looks like Garrett is going to pull through. I'm thankful that I'm not losing Dad, and he didn't lose me.

-Daniel

## April 17

He woke up.

Garrett's mom said the first thing he said was, "Get this shit off me!" He had no idea where he was and made a huge scene. I wish I was there to see it. Not to hold it against him or anything, but to see him cursing and swinging at the nurses.

I can breathe again knowing that he's going to be okay.

-Daniel

## April 19

I'm skipping classes to go see Garrett. My anxiety has kept me from going sooner, and the insurance didn't release the rental car until yesterday for some reason. Hospitals are giant cesspools anyway and I've already been in that hospital way too many times this year. That makes me sound like a pansy.

-Daniel

---

I managed to make it to Garrett's room without touching anything. Between the automatic sliding glass doors and other people pushing the elevator buttons, I'm feeling a little impressed with myself. I shove my hands deep into my pockets and slowly peek into his hospital room. Garrett's mom is looking at her phone and he is passed out.

Maybe I should have called first, I don't want to wake him. I hesitate and take a step back, right into a nurse.

"Oof." She places her hands on my shoulders to steady me. "Careful."

"Sorry."

Garrett's mom jumps up. "Daniel!" She rushes over to hug me, my hands still in my pockets. "I was wondering when you were going to stop by."

"Wake up sleepy head, you have a visitor." The nurse picks up the clipboard from the foot of the bed. "How are you feeling today?"

"Wha?" Garrett barely moves. "Aren't there visiting hours or something?"

"Daniel is family," his mom says.

"Daniel!" Garrett's eyes fly open as he tries to sit up.

"Oh no, don't do that." The nurse gently pushes him back down.

Garrett's mom gives me one more awkward hug, "Shouldn't you be in school?"

I promptly nod, half hoping between her and the nurse they'd kick me out because I can't stop staring at the needles protruding out of the top of Garrett's hand, surrounded by lumpy, angry stitches that look like they're threatening to snap at any moment. I glance up to his face, covered in nicks and scratches, followed by his shaved stitch-covered head. I don't remember all of these injuries the night of the accident. How could I have not noticed he was this bad?

It's one thing hearing how bad he was from my parents, but finally seeing it in person? My stomach hurts. My skin is crawling. My mind can't decide if I need to gather my best friend up in a hug and carry him out of this place, or run home straight to my shower to scrub my skin off.

"You can talk to him you know," the nurse whispers over my shoulder and pushes a chair towards me.

"You guys catch up, I have some phone calls to make, and some coffee to drink." Garrett's mom says and walks toward the door.

"Thanks, Mom." Garrett's attempt at a smile is ruined by the cut over his lip. Like the creepy version of the Joker. And the Joker is creepy enough.

I've never heard Garrett thank his mom in my life. The life-and-death-ness of this whole situation hits me again and I sink into the empty chair, my hands still in my pockets.

The room clears out and it's just me and Garrett. I can't even look at him. Not because of his injuries this time, but because of consuming guilt. And maybe a little blame for him being so late the night of the accident.

"You don't think I'm pretty anymore, do you?" Garrett bats his eyelashes.

My mouth forces a grin without my consent. "Chicks dig scars. And you're going to have a shit load of them."

"Hells yeah. You should see the one on my chest." He moves for a moment, then gives up. "I'll show you later."

I pull my hands out of my pockets and study them. How is it possible that we were both in the same accident and I came out mostly fine, and he looks like he fell in a garbage disposal? I shove my hands back into my pockets. They feel safer in there.

"I'm glad you're okay." The words sound a bit shallow coming out of my mouth.

"I'm glad you're okay."

I shrug. "I don't look like I just survived hand-to-hand combat with a knife-wielding ninja."

"I've been through worse." We both let out a laugh before shutting up. Because we both know that's unfortunately true.

I study the giant boot on his foot and cringe. I wonder if it'll affect his prospects in soccer. He wanted to play soccer in college. My body sinks deeper into the chair. This really sucks. All of it. "Do you know how long you'll be in that boot?"

Garrett responds with a snore.

I watch his chest shakily rise and fall until his shallow snoring turns into a deep consistent rhythm that reminds me of the ocean. The pain buried into lines across his forehead smooth out. Tears sneak up behind my eyes and wait for permission to fall out.

It's crazy how close he was to death. It's crazy how we both were. He lingered at the gates a bit longer though. I'm glad he's sticking around. I don't know if I could keep moving forward without my brother.

## April 30

I'm seeing Dr. Hannah today for the first time since the accident. I thought I would be nervous about it, but I'm not. It's weirdly comforting knowing that he will know exactly what to say. Well, most of the time he knows what to say. Hopefully today won't be the exception.

-Daniel

———

"You've been to hell and back. How are you coping?" Dr. Hannah flips open his notebook and sits in a chair across from me.

"It's weird, like my brain is a strange swirl of relief and panic. I have this need to sit back and rest from all the crazy that's been happening, but also like the hummingbird has taken flight all over my body, leaving me feeling exhausted. If I think about what happened to Garrett too much, I feel like I need to run through my rituals like my brain thinks it can fix it. Go back in time to stop it from happening. But that's being balanced by the relief of knowing that he's alive, and it's because I overcame a genuine fear."

"That's a well thought out conclusion."

"It's stupid that I almost let my OCD take over in a life-and-death situation. How can something like that have so much control over me?"

"You can't help that. When the chemicals in our brains are out of balance, we rarely have a hundred percent control over our thoughts."

"No, but I should have been able to override those thoughts and gone into action sooner." A little more guilt trickles in.

"We never know how we will react in these situations. The mind is a complicated ball of fat and neurons. The fight or flight or freeze mechanism is a stronger force than most people realize."

"But I froze. And that almost cost my best friend his life."

"And it still would not have been your fault." Dr. Hannah's words are stern.

Wouldn't it have been? My body is perfectly capable, but it was my brain that made me hesitate. If it wasn't for my brain stopping me from helping Garrett after the car accident, wouldn't I have been able to jump into action sooner? Maybe he would have been in better shape now if my brain didn't get in the way with all the thoughts. Stupid thoughts that pushed their way in without my permission.

"I just don't know how someone with OCD can continue to cope in such a messy world. This whole year has been shit, my whole life fell apart. Sometimes the only thing I can focus on is my own spiral, how am I supposed to grow and move on if I can't always focus outward?"

Dr. Hannah lets out a heavy sigh. "It is a struggle. An impossible one, it sometimes seems. But you proved that you're stronger than your OCD in many ways already. Even when everything gets messy."

"It's just so exhausting."

"It is. And it's possible that it will continue to feel exhausting for a long time. Until you find a new balance and routine again. I just want you to know that you are not alone in this. You have me, and I know both of your parents don't want you to feel like you're struggling through your OCD on your own, either."

I nod. I know he's right. But I still can't help feeling like I'm alone in this. I make everyone's lives more difficult because of my problems.

"And I don't want you to feel like you're a burden, Daniel."

I look up and stare at him. Of course he can read minds too.

He laughs. "I've been doing this long enough to know when people's minds start to wander. You're counting subconsciously with your fingers."

I glance down at my right hand tapping out a four beat on my chest. "Oh." I quickly ball my hand into a fist and let it drop into my lap.

"You know, that's not a bad habit to have. It helps you calm down, and it's not hurting anyone. And also, importantly, it's not hurting you, either. I don't want to stop the helpful or neutral ticks you may have. Just the negative intrusive thoughts, and the ticks that are hurting you, physically and mentally. Or the rituals that are taking up all your time and energy. Those are the things we want to stop. Not the habits you've formed to help calm you down. Especially not the ones that are not harming yourself."

I relax my hand and flex my fingers. "Yeah." It's not hurting me. Counting does help calm me down. I smile to myself as another wave of relief flows over me.

"Counting only becomes a problem when it becomes the center of your focus and takes up too much time. Moving it from a coping mechanism, into a negative cycle."

"Where's the balance?"

"Is it consuming your thoughts? Or helping you refocus?"

I nod.

"Daniel, you need to know, if you have the courage to overcome OCD to save your friend's life, you have the courage to overcome it to save your own life too. I'm really proud of you."

I don't know what to say. A weight slides off my shoulders and dissipates in front of me. For the first time since I've started therapy this year, I finally feel like I'm moving forward. Like OCD isn't going to win this time.

**May 15**

Garrett is home today. I went with Mom to pick him up because his mom's car isn't working. It was another slap of reality being in his home again. The last time I was there was elementary school. It's small, dark, and hadn't been dusted in forever. There wasn't much food in his cabinets either. Ever since then, Garrett always came over to my house. He never minded it. He said he would rather hang out at my place anyways because I had Nintendo and cookies.

My mom bought groceries and filled up their kitchen. His mom was embarrassed. Honestly, I was glad to get out of there. It looked exactly the same from when I was there all those years ago. Mom volunteered to keep Garrett at our house until he was up and moving better, but his mom was upset she even asked. Mom settled on taking him to his physical therapy appointments instead. I know she wasn't trying to insult Garrett's mom. We all know how tight things are for them, and she wants to make sure he's taken care of. It would have been awesome to have him staying with us again, though.

-Daniel

## May 17

Dad texted me last night to ask when I'm going to come and see his new place. I'm not ready for this to be real, but if I stay in this house another minute today with Mom, one of us is bound to blow our lid. I can't handle all of this change right now, but she's been ready for it for years.

I guess I've failed to get on board until now. Well, I wouldn't say I'm even on board now… but being dragged behind.

-Daniel

I pull into a visitor parking spot in the parking garage next to Dad's new apartment. This makes it official, I guess. Visiting his new place kind of drives the last remaining nail in the coffin of this mess. There's no way I can be in denial after I see his new place. His place. Not our place. Not Mom and Dad's place… But his.

With my shoulder I push open a set of double glass doors connecting the parking garage to the apartments. Stiff, deep blue carpet runs down a long hall with small mailboxes lining the walls. At the end, three separate elevators. The shiny silver doors showing me my reflection. I push my hair out of my face before hitting the up button, trying not to think about how many other people have already touched that button today. The doors slide open. Then slide closed.

Shit. I squeeze my eyes shut and hit the button again. This time I step into the elevator and hit the button for the twelfth floor. When the doors open again, I shove my hands deep into my pockets and wander down the hall to find Dad's door. The teal door with a gold 12D in the middle stands out against the blank white walls.

The door is slightly off the latch. Do I still knock? Just walk in? Why is this so weird? I roll my eyes at myself. He's my dad, this shouldn't bring me this much anxiety. I pull in a deep breath that fills my lungs to the bottom, and decide to knock and walk in at the same time.

"Hello?" I take my shoes off in the miniature foyer and latch the door behind me. Maybe I should have stayed in the hall?

"You made it! I was worried you might have gotten lost." Dad drops the box he was carrying and grabs me up in a bear hug. "I'm so glad you came. Come on in, have a seat."

I look around the light and airy apartment. A line of floor to ceiling windows cover the far wall. A grey couch sits in front of them. No curtains. No other seating in the room. I walk past the small eat-in kitchen, which also has no seating, and drop onto the couch.

The apartment is still a disaster, plastic trash bags and boxes scattered everywhere.

"Yeah, don't look at the mess. I haven't had a lot of time to get settled yet."

I shrug. "There's been a lot going on." I squish the soft carpet under my feet. It's almost white. So clean. How long until it ends up with a big red wine stain on it?

"Oh! I have a surprise for you." Dad pushes a few boxes to the side of the wall in the hallway and motions for me to follow.

He opens the first door on the right, into a comfortably sized empty room.

"Nice... Your office?" I examine another set of floor-to-ceiling windows, looking straight into the building across the street. "You should really get curtains for this place."

"I should. I already scared some child across the way in my boxer shorts yesterday. It was not a pretty sight. And no, not my office. Your room! I figured it might be nice to have a place to come on school breaks and weekends. If you wanted."

"School breaks? Try full time. With everything that happened this year, I forgot to submit my college applications. Maybe I can try over the summer and get in for the January semester or something. Maybe... I don't know." My heart slams into my chest at the thought that I just ruined my entire future.

"What are you talking about?"

I shrug. If I think about it too much, I might have a meltdown in my new empty room.

Dad's eyes narrow as he rubs his chin. Then they grow wide and he covers his mouth. "Dammit. Hold on just a minute." He disappears down the hall. The sounds of rustling papers and boxes being kicked fill the room.

I walk over to the wall of windows and lean my forehead on them, trying to see down to the street. Twelve stories feels higher than it sounds. At least I'll have a room with a... I slowly look back at the building across the street. At least the architecture is interesting.

"For some reason, I thought I already gave this to you. I must have shoved it in a box instead. I already opened it and read it, because I didn't want to give it to you in case it was bad news." Dad hands me the opened envelope.

I grab it from him, the emblem of the state university ten minutes' walk from here is embossed on the front of the envelope. I can't help but crack a smile.

"Garrett asked me for help applying. He wanted to stay close to home to keep an eye on his siblings. And I thought, what the hell. Garrett stole an essay from last year out of your desk. It wasn't hard. You keep everything so organized."

"Did he get in?"

"You'll have to ask him." His smile grows wide.

I nod. Of course he got in. I pull out the piece of paper, and proceed to read my acceptance letter.

"I put undeclared for your major. I was kind of hoping, maybe you wanted to join the family business." He winks.

"Gross. No way. I'm sorry Dad, but no way am I touching other people's feet."

He laughs. "I figured, but a man can dream."

I shove the acceptance letter into my back pocket and throw my arms around him. "Thanks, Dad." Relief flows out of me. Maybe everything will be okay.

His breath rustles through my hair as he squeezes me one more time before letting go. "I was thinking, maybe we can go pick out a new bedroom set to fill this space. What do you think?"

I nod, and finally accept the realization—the *truth,* that he's still going to be my dad, no matter what. That adoption means forever. I stand a little taller, and take comfort that this is one relationship I never have to worry about losing again. "I think that sounds amazing."

## May 20

I'm eighteen today. It feels so weird. Both Mom and Dad told me they would do something with me separately next month. I think the other one assumed the other was going to do something today...

Garrett's coming over to my house after school today instead. I told him I could come to him, but he said I have better food at my house. It's going to be a harsh new reality when he comes over and discovers Mom hasn't cooked in a while. I've taken to eating oatmeal bars, cheese, and apples. For every meal. A person can only handle so much pizza. And after the last delivery guy, I'm starting to question the pizza place's hygiene policy...

-Daniel

———

Through my bedroom window I spot Garrett hobbling down the street. His lopsided walk only emphasizes the large walking boot on his foot. A small backpack is slung over his free shoulder. His other arm? Thrown in a sling and strapped to his chest.

I run down the stairs and fling open the front door, half jogging down the sidewalk to meet him. "You could have at least let me come and pick you up. Dad got me a rental until we find a new car."

"And miss out on this chance to exercise? No way man, my sad ass needs extra encouragement. Oh hey, and happy birthday, bastard."

"Thanks." Guilt sneaks up on me as I remember I forgot his birthday earlier this year… But instead of bringing that up, I roll my eyes, grab his backpack and hold it under my arm. I'm not sure if I should grab his arm and help him or not. I'm too afraid to try, or ask. He's liable to land a fist in the center of my face for treating him like an old woman.

We finally make it to the front door. It took even longer than I thought it would. "You should at least let me drive you home later. I have that rental…"

"No thanks. I'm avoiding all forms of motorized transportation right now. Except buses. There is a smaller chance of getting flung out of them." Garrett makes his way straight to the kitchen.

"But a bigger chance of getting mugged." I drop my body on the couch, his bag on the floor next to me, and wait for him to come back from the kitchen.

He quietly makes his way back into the living room and kicks an empty box that's in his way. "What the hell man? Does your mom not love us any more or something?" He carefully sits in the chair across from me. "I've never seen that fridge so fucking empty before."

"We can get food later. She left me cash."

He crosses his free arm over his stomach. "Totally not the same. I guess it really is almost the end of an era."

"Speaking of the end of an era… I heard we got into the same university?"

"Oh yeah!" Garrett sits up too fast and quickly regrets it as he winces and sits back into the chair. "I put you down to be my roommate. You'll do the same?"

I nod. "I can't believe you guys did that."

"Brick walls can do more than stop you from being a dickhead, you know. Toss me my bag?"

I get up and hand it to him. I don't trust his catching abilities right now. He pulls out a small bottle and unscrews the cap and pulls out a dropper, dropping a few drops of liquid under his tongue.

"What is that?" I squint, trying to read the bottle.

"CBD oil, motherfucker."

I cross my arms and look down at him.

"Sit the hell down, man. You can't get high off this shit. I kept throwing up the pain meds from the hospital and ripping out stitches. So my doctor suggested I try this instead. And it's natural."

"Cyanide is natural."

He rolls his eyes. "Out of all the things in my life you could be judging me for, you pick this? It's not even illegal."

I pause. He's right. He's done a lot of stupid shit.

"Hey, don't think about that too hard."

"Does it work?" I ask and finally back off.

"It takes the edge off. Not like the hard-core stuff would. But I don't like feeling all numb and dizzy from the pain meds anyway. Which was the other side effect when I could keep them down."

"What are you hungry for?"

He shrugs. "Whatever."

"Chinese?"

"Dude, I fucking love MSG."

I frown. Now I don't want cheap Chinese food. At least most of the stuff I usually order is fried, so I know all of the germs definitely die in the high heat.

Garrett stands up and walks to the kitchen. "Seriously, don't think about it too hard, Chinese sounds great." He hands me a stack of menus out of the junk drawer.

I dial and order the same things I always get.

"Kung pao chicken!" Garrett shouts into the phone.

I add that to the order and hang up. "It'll be here in an hour."

"Sweet. I'm starving."

"Apple?"

"Fuck no, son. I can wait."

"Nintendo?"

"Yes please. It's been a while since I've kicked your ass."

"You have one hand."

He follows me into the den and slowly drops himself into an overstuffed chair. "Yeah, and when I beat you, you'll feel like a dumbass."

"No, I'll feel like a dumbass when I kick your ass because you're an invalid and it won't feel right. So I'm just going to let you win so you have something to look forward to."

He clicks his tongue. "Man. Shut the fuck up and turn that thing on. I'm Mario."

"You're always Mario."

"Cause I'm the boss."

Normal. I forgot what it felt like to feel normal. "Okay, boss. Let's go!" I hit play and we're ten again. We zone out until the doorbell rings and our food arrives. Almost two hours later.

"Not your mom's food, but still good. If you like that fried, over-sauced kind of thing." Garret shoves a huge chunk of kung pao chicken into his mouth.

We stuff our faces in silence for at least fifteen minutes before Garrett gets up and disappears down the hall. I grab another container and pop the lid open.

"Mmm." I breathe in the oily smell of fried rice and take a huge bite.

Garrett hobbles back down the hall, kicking a Costco-size package of toilet paper with his one good foot. "Dude, you guys are prepared for a zombie apocalypse. You're never going to run out of toilet paper. I never knew you could buy this much at once."

"What are you doing?" I place the box of fried rice on the floor next to me and stand up. "Do you need help wiping your ass too?"

"Oh, you think you're funny now, do you?"

I smile and shrug. "Seriously, what are you doing?"

"Okay, hear me out." Garrett turns the box of toilet paper on its side and sits on it. "It's your birthday, so we need to do something big."

"It's my eighteenth birthday, so it'll make it easier for me to go to jail. So, no."

"You don't even know what I was going to say."

"Do I have to?"

"Man, shut up and listen."

I cross my arms over my chest and wait for an answer.

"Just think of it as a form of therapy."

"I don't even know what you're wanting to do yet."

He smiles wide. "We should TP someone's house."

"Ha." I leave him in the hall to walk back into the den and grab my fried rice. "Come sit down so I can beat you again."

"You clearly have a strong advantage. And I really wouldn't be bragging about beating a one-armed man." He kicks the huge box of TP into the den.

I ignore him and start another game, this time by myself. Halfway through I die and turn to see Garrett staring at me. My heart jumps to my throat. This is going to happen. He is going to make it happen. I sigh and rub my face. "Whose house?"

"Kayla's." His smile turns sinister.

My heart jumps higher. "No. No fucking way. Fuck no. That's a terrible idea, Garrett!"

"It's a wonderful idea."

"What if she sees us? Or her parents call the cops on us?"

"It's almost midnight, they'll probably be asleep anyway."

"What about you? What am I supposed to strap you on my back and carry you along while I do all the work?"

"Hey! That's not a half-bad idea." His smile gets even wider. "You know you want to."

"Carry you around like an overgrown toddler?"

"No, fucker, TP Kayla's house. She did you dirty. There has to be some part of you that wants a little... Retribution?"

"No." I finish off the fried rice and reach for the last egg roll.

"Well, I do. Support your best friend. I've always supported you."

"Not true." I pick up the empty take out containers and head towards the kitchen. Garrett follows, kicking the giant box, slowly, one unsure step at a time.

"Okay, fair. We went through a rough patch for a while... but we've grown and moved on. Right?"

"I don't know, I'm feeling like we're about to hit another rough patch soon." I wipe down the already bare countertops with a clean rag and put the few dirty dishes in the sink into the dishwasher. Then wash my hands before folding my arms across my chest again. Garrett quirks an eyebrow and stares back. A stand-off.

After a few moments of silence, Garrett shrugs. "Fine, lil' fucker. Have it your way. You can stay here and spend the rest of your birthday being a goody two-shoes and following the rules. I'm going to go have fun." He kicks the huge box of toilet paper towards the back door, opens it with his good hand, leans against the door with his hip, and with his good foot, attempts to kick the box out the door. Instead it gets stuck between the boot on his other foot and the door jam.

He attempts to pull his booted foot free, and accidentally pulls the box back with it, causing him to spin and stumble, falling butt-first right onto the box.

My heart jumps in my chest and I run over to him. "Are you okay?"

He pops his bottom lip out. "If I say no, will you take me to Kayla's?"

I sigh. "Shit, Garrett. Fine."

"Fuck yeah!" He jumps up and winces as he knocks his slinged arm on the doorknob on the way up.

"This is a terrible idea."

"Totally."

I roll my eyes and grab my car keys off the hook by the door and freeze. The cold keys in my hands feel like stones that weigh a thousand pounds.

"Have you driven since the accident?" Garrett asks.

"Yeah. I took the rental to the hospital to see you that one time. But I haven't driven with anybody yet. I get a little jumpy whenever I'm riding with my parents sometimes. You?"

He shrugs. "You know I mostly take the bus. We could walk? It's like ten minutes from here, right?"

"With your sorry ass? No way. It's thirty-plus minutes on foot. Longer with you dragging along."

"Take the bus?"

My skin crawls and I instantly have the urge to vomit. A germ-infested bus runs through my mind, carrying a load of human zombies freshly infected with Ebola. "It doesn't run late on this side of town."

"Figures. Bunch of yuppies."

I can't handle his disappointment. I should just drive. "Idea!" I drop the keys on the counter and run out the kitchen door to the garage. I flip the lights on and stare at the massive mound of packing boxes and push them over to one side.

"Uh, what? An idea?" Garrett kicks the box of TP to the side of the door and leans against the garage door.

"I get those sometimes." Where is it? I push more boxes over to the side until I spot a shiny red corner covered in dust. "Ah!" I grab it and pull out a little red wagon.

"Fuck, yes." Garrett breathes in as his eyes grow wide. He practically prances over to me, and with his free hand helps move a few more boxes to free the little red wagon.

We drag it out of the garage together and I wipe my dusty hands on my pants. Dusty pants. My hands feel grimy. "Hold on."

"Mmhhmm." He continues to stare at the wagon wide-eyed.

I run into the house and wash my hands in the sink. And join Garrett back outside again. No, no I have to change my pants. I run back inside and up the stairs to my room and pull out a new pair of pants. I should shower first. I pull off the dusty pants and toss them in the hamper and turn on the shower, then promptly turn it off. "Stop." I feel gross. I feel dry and crusty and germy. But am I really?

Yes. I reach for the shower faucet again and freeze.

I feel like I am, but I am not. Not really. I pull in a deep breath and hold it, quickly putting on the clean pants, and for good measure, a clean shirt too. Then wash my hands again and run back outside to Garrett.

"I'm surprised you didn't take a whole damn shower." Garrett looks up at me from the little red wagon. "I had enough time to dust this thing again, then get myself stuck." He attempts to stand back up but quickly gives up. "I was almost afraid I would never see you again because your showers take ten thousand years and archaeologists would have found my fucking bones stuck in this tiny ass wagon."

I bust up laughing and offer him my hand.

He pushes it away. "Come on, fucker, I'm already in this thing. Let's get the hell out of here!"

I grab the box and drop it on this lap and grab the handle of the wagon.

Garrett hugs the box with his free arm, grinning ear to ear.

This is totally normal. I won't end up in jail at all by the end of the night. Not at all...

"Start the engine!" Garrett kicks his boot in the air.

I pull the wagon out of the driveway. "Holy shit, you're a lot heavier than you look!"

"It's called muscle, dude, and the ladies love it." Ge flexes his arm and kisses his bicep. "Now quit your bitchin' and get to rollin'!"

It's midnight by the time we make it to Kayla's house, and all the lights are out. I pull the wagon into some bushes on the side of the house. My arms and legs are throbbing. My heart is already on a high-speed chase around my rib cage. We sit in silence and stare at the dark street in front of us.

Garrett pushes the box off and attempts to get out of the wagon. I offer him my hand again, and he slaps it away.

"Okay." I take a step back and watch him struggle to get out of the wagon with one arm and one functioning foot. Finally he rolls to his side, and both he and the wagon fall over and he awkwardly stands back up.

"See? I got it." He grins. "So, how do you want to do this?"

I cock my head to the side and give him a side-eye. "This was your idea. You didn't think we'd ever get this far, did you?"

"Fuck no. I was expecting you to stick hardcore to your straitlaced ways, Mr. Goody Two-shoes. Or give up about halfway over here, because that shit was way longer than thirty minutes."

"I mean, yeah." I rub both of my screaming arms.

"Okay, game plan. If they come outside, you'll just have to leave me in the bushes. Book it back to your house, get the car, and come back for me in the morning."

"Good plan." I open the box and pull out the first roll of toilet paper.

"I mean, neither of us has ever done anything like this before, if we turn back now, no one would even know. Plus, you know, I'm a fucking invalid."

I laugh at Garrett's sudden onset of insecurity. I'm not sure if he actually thought through the possibility of me actually saying yes. "All bark, no bite."

"Oh hell no. I'm no lapdog." He grabs his own roll. "Fuck you."

"If my parents find out—"

"If your parents find out, what? They'll stop loving you?"

That line hits me between the eyes. That's always been a huge fear of mine, that I do something they didn't like and they would hate me, Dad would leave… but he's already left, and he still loves me. "I guess not."

"They'd probably be glad that you did something on your birthday and had fun."

"This feels more like anxiety and anticipation of a prison sentence than fun right now." I clear my throat.

"Now who's all bark and no bite? Girl did you dirty. Remember?" Garrett hands me another roll of TP and smiles that sinister smile of his.

I swallow my heart back down into my ribcage and tap out a quick run on my chest before grabbing an arm-full of rolls from the box. I want to be prepared. Eight rolls. Four for him, four for me. "You ready?"

"I'm your fucking brick wall, baby. I'm was born ready."

He kicks the wagon further into the bushes and I follow him into Kayla's yard. I want to run, but I'm with an invalid. I drop the rolls by the base of a large tree in front of Kayla's house and pick up my first roll.

"Holy shit." Garrett whispers and tosses his roll into the tree in the middle of her yard. I follow suit and toss my roll into the same tree.

My anxiety flies through the air, wraps around a branch and flows back down towards me. Only it's not anxiety that returns. It's freedom. Not freedom from Kayla, but freedom from the steel-bolted box I've kept myself in all these years. I toss it up again around another branch. Garrett hobbles around throwing his roll as high as he could get it with his free non-dominant hand, then hurries out of the way so it wouldn't hit him on the way down.

We toss two more rolls into the tree and start wrapping the bushes in TP, then tossing the nearly-done rolls over the roof of the house. I run back to the wagon and grab a few more rolls.

"It looks awesome." Garrett tosses his new roll all over the yard.

"Yeah it does." Like everything from the past is being washed away, made pure again. I smile wide until my cheeks hurt. I can't believe I let him talk me into this.

"Hey, pack up, tuck tail, and run." Garrett grabs my arm.

"Why? We still have a lot of TP in the box."

"Because that's why." He points to a car turning the corner down the street.

"Oh shit." We drop our rolls, and I wrap my arm around Garrett's waist and half drag him into the bushes on the side of the house. The car pulls into Kayla's driveway.

"Ohh…" Garrett half laughs.

"Really?" My heart jumps out of my chest and races down the road. Shit, shit, shit, shit! This was such a bad idea, why did I let him talk me into this? I try to stand up, ready to turn myself in as Garrett grabs my hand and yanks me back down.

"I forgot Kayla's dad works the late shift. I used to work for him a couple years ago," Garrett whispers.

"You forgot?"

"Dude, you're the one who was dating his daughter. How could you not know?"

I click my tongue and elbow him on the side. "Shut up. We're going to jail." In through my nose, and out through my mouth. I tap in counts of four on my now hollow chest.

Garrett giggles before slapping his hand over his mouth. We

watch as Kayla's dad slowly gets out of his car and wanders into his front yard with his hands on his hips.

"He's admiring our work," Garrett says quietly. "How sweet."

Kayla's dad shakes his head and heads back towards the side door of his house. As soon as I hear the door close, I jump up. "I'm going to get the car, you stay here."

"No, I'm coming with you."

I sigh and rub my face. Regretting it instantly as my hands were just in the dirt. I wipe my hands on my pants and push the thoughts down.

"Stop thinking so hard and help me up."

I help Garrett up and he gets back in the wagon just as the light in the living room turns on and the curtains open.

"Fuck!" Garrett rolls right back out of the wagon and onto the ground. He yanks me down again and I join him in the dirt behind the bushes.

"This was a terrible idea!" I try not to shout.

"Yeah, and I agreed with you! Don't fucking act like this was all my fault! You had a good fucking hour of dragging my ass behind you to change your mind!"

"All this because you hate Kayla?"

"All this because she was an asshole! To YOU! And me. But mostly you! And a lot to me, but that's beside the point!"

"I can sneak off and get the car without him seeing me. If I run it'll take less than twenty minutes. I'll come back and get you, you jump into the back and I'll speed off. He won't even see us." I get back up on my knees. Kayla's dad is still there. Staring out the window. His hands on his hips. "Shit. What if he knows?"

"Knows what?"

"That it was me?"

"He would never guess that." Garrett giggles again. "I mean… Maybe he would, actually."

"You sound like a little girl."

"Yeah, and you sound like you got your balls in a vice. We go back together. I'm pretty sure he can't see over here anyway. I'll jump in the wagon and help you roll it back to the sidewalk and you run us down to the corner."

"All of your ideas tonight are terrible!" I rub my face in my hands again and let out a frustrated sigh, then wipe my face with the hem of my shirt instead.

"On three."

"Wait, no—"

Garrett gets up. "One." Drops himself in the wagon—

"No!"

"Two." Starts pulling himself into position—

"Garrett!"

"Three!" He yells and rolls off into the middle of the sidewalk and sits there stranded.

"Fuck!" I grab an armful of loose toilet paper rolls and drop them into his lap before grabbing the handle of the wagon and running down the street as fast as I can go.

"Ahh!" we both scream as soon as we make it down the street and turn the corner.

"Shit, do you think he saw us?" I'm still screaming. My blood pressure is still rising.

"I don't know, maybe?"

"Because you were fucking yelling!"

"You were fucking yelling!"

"Ahhh!" I scream louder as a truck speeds past us. "Shit!" I pause and grab my chest, concentrating on pulling in a few breaths.

A crack of lightning shoots across the sky.

"Shit, did you know it was going to rain?" Garrett asks.

"Oh no." I shake my head. "That's bad, isn't it?"

He nods, then busts up laughing. "Now she can't use that TP to wipe her tears as she cleans it up tomorrow!"

"I kind of feel bad." I shrug.

"Dude. You'll feel even worse if we get caught in the rain."

"Shit, Garrett!" I grip the wagon handle tighter and run down the sidewalk. In the dark. With Garrett hugging several rolls of loose toilet paper in his lap. A couple rolls fall out, leaving a trail behind us.

"Faster! We're going to get soaked!" Garrett yells.

A few drops of rain fall from the sky and land on my face. "I'm going as fast as I can!" My muscles in my shoulders and calves burn with every step. The rain picks up a little more as I make it to my street, and finally begins to pour as I pull Garrett into the driveway.

I pull him out of the wagon and we nearly trip over each other to get into the kitchen, dumping the soaked TP rolls on the floor.

"What in the world...?" Mom looks up from a glass of wine and a book at the kitchen counter.

We both freeze.

"Where the hell have you been?" She puts the book down and stares at the soggy rolls on the floor. "You know what. I don't even want to know. I don't want to feel guilty if anyone asks. You could have at least left a note or brought your phone with you."

"Sorry. Totally my fault." Garrett raises his hand.

"All his fault." I agree with him and he elbows me in the side.

"Oh, and we're out of toilet paper," he adds.

"Hmm." Mom takes a sip from her wine glass and looks us up and down again. "Well, I hope you had fun." She walks over and kisses me on the shoulder. "But if a police officer ends up knocking on the front door in a few minutes, I'm handing you two over."

"That's fair," Garrett says. "To be honest, I'm an invalid though, and you should probably take pity on me."

It's my turn to elbow him in the side.

Mom rolls her eyes. "Happy birthday, Daniel. Clean up your mess." She motions to the water and lumpy TP rolls. "I'm going to bed. You both have school in a few hours."

"You're not mad?" My voice quakes.

"Of course I'm mad. But it's also your birthday so I can't yell at you until later."

"Technically it's not his birthday anymore. That was yesterday." Garrett grins.

"Man, shut up," I spit out.

"I bought stuff to make you breakfast when you wake up. Love you, good night." Mom kisses my other shoulder and disappears down the hall.

"Holy fuck." Garrett breathes out as soon as we hear her door shut. "She's really going to make us go to school tomorrow? Worst birthday ever."

I grin. "I disagree. Best birthday ever. Now I'm going to go shower. Want the cot, or couch?"

"Couch. Night." He grins back.

## May 21

I feel like shit. Also happy, for the first time in a long time—I couldn't stop smiling all morning. But trying to function on so little sleep is keeping my head sloshy.

This morning when I woke up, I was stiff and buzzy. Mom made us a huge breakfast though, and gave me a birthday present. A new journal, and a day planner. Both perfect for the start of a new chapter.

I managed to drive Garrett to school without either of us freaking out. I was a bit jumpy, he fell asleep and I had to wake him up once we got to school. Garrett went straight to the counselor's office to play catch up, and I went and helped with grad set up with the rest of the seniors.

That's a lie. I sat in a chair zoning out while everyone else was working. Shayla Jacobsen, the official valedictorian, asked me to give a speech. She said the class voted and wants me to be one of the speakers. Shayla said that I was an 'inspiration.' I hate that. I'm not an inspiration, I've been trying to not drown all year. There's nothing inspirational about that. Maybe they just want a feel-good story. I told her no, but she asked me to think about it, that everyone else was still on my side.

How could they be after I blocked everyone out this year? I ditched all my friends and stopped trying. A lot of them stopped trying too, but I don't blame them. I get it.

I don't know. Maybe I will think about it. Maybe it's something I need to do. For closure, to help me move on.

-Daniel

I lean against my car in the parking lot to Dr. Hannah's office. It's almost relieving to know that I'm going to be staying in town for school this fall. I won't have to find another therapist. I rub my face and accept the possibility of seeing therapists off-and-on until I'm dead. There are worse fates. And Dr. Hannah's starting to grow on me.

"Hello, Daniel!" Dr. Hannah walks across the parking lot, holding a large Slurpee cup. "You're early."

"Yeah, I left school a little early... Everyone's doing grad set up stuff. There wasn't a lot for me to do." There wasn't a lot I wanted to do.

"It's exciting that you're graduating so soon! Well, come on in."

I follow him into his office and check in with the secretary.

He takes a seat at his desk and digs the palm of his hand into his eye. "Brain freeze."

I take a seat in my usual spot. He shoves his thumb into his mouth and rubs the roof of his mouth, then wipes his thumb into his pants before taking another gulp from his Slurpee.

"Well, shall we begin?" Dr. Hannah smiles and takes a pen and notebook out of his drawer.

I nod. I hope he knows I'm not shaking his hand after that.

"How have your meds been treating you?"

"Good. Nothing to complain about."

He nods and jots something down. "You do seem to be in a good mood."

"Yeah, I am. Sore, but good."

"Sore?"

"Oh, working out..." A grin slides across my face.

"Good for you! Physical exercise is really good for helping to quiet the mind. I like some good ol' tai chi myself."

I nod and fold my hands in my lap.

"Is there anything specific you wanted to talk about today?"

"Not really…"

"Okay, do you mind if I take the reins?"

"No objection." He's really good at that. Not in a negative way, but in the "I never know where to start, because every time I walk into his office my brain goes blank" kind of way.

"How have you been doing with resisting those compulsions of yours recently?"

"I think I've been doing okay. I mean I haven't been perfect or anything." Images from last night float through my mind. There was plenty of opportunity for my mind to stop me, and it almost did, but I managed to push through and ended up having a lot of fun.

"Oh, it's not going to be perfect for a while, if at all. But the more you stand up to your brain, the easier it will be to recognize those feelings that are trying to bring you down into a spiral."

I nod. "Those spirals though…" Then sigh. "Sometimes I don't even realize I'm in one until I'm already at the bottom and can't get out."

"That's when you call your support team, if you can."

"Team." That word used to hold so much weight. Now it tastes a little bitter in my mouth.

"Yeah, like your mom, dad, friends, etcetera."

"Friend." I smile to myself and rub my sore arms.

"Three is a pretty solid team. Plus you equals four! All the tires you need for a car."

"Plus a spare in case you have an accident."

He smiles wide. "That would be me."

I laugh. "Okay. Yeah." I guess that is a pretty solid team.

"You really are having a good day."

"I feel a little like the old me today."

"No, the new you. The older and wiser you. Never go backward, always forward. You've learned a lot about yourself recently, more than most people do in a lifetime."

"I don't feel like I have." My smile fades a bit. "I feel like I went backward."

"Impossible. You've never faced your parents going through a divorce before. You thought you wouldn't survive that, but look at you, you did. You moved past that feeling and that false truth and came out the other side. What did you learn about your parent's divorce?"

My stomach sinks. It still hurts like hell. "That it didn't kill me. It felt like it did though. But I'm pretty sure I'll survive now."

"Why?"

"Because I'm not losing my dad like I thought I would. And... it's not my fault."

"What's not your fault?"

"My parent's divorce."

"Why isn't it your fault?"

My smile returns a little, I see what he's getting at. "Because I can't control other people and their actions."

"And?"

"My compulsions won't change the outcome of other people's decisions even if I think they will. Because my feelings don't always match up with reality."

"Whoa!" Dr. Hannah shouts. "Breakthrough! I wasn't

expecting you to take it that far, but good for you! I'm proud of you, Daniel." He writes down a few notes. "When was the last time you did your rituals?"

"Oh." I don't know, I haven't thought about them for a while. I don't have a clue when those dropped out. I shrug. "I really can't remember." I did my morning ritual every morning for years, it's strange that I can't remember.

"Hmm." He clicks his pen. "Why do you think that is?"

I shrug again. "I don't know. I think I was doing them to keep everything calm and everyone happy at home. But obviously that didn't work."

"Why is that?"

"Because my feelings don't always match up with reality..."

"True. Remember, and keep practicing, when you have a big emotion or negative feeling pop up, check and see if it's reality. If not, tell it to stop, picture that big red stop sign if you need to, then replace it with a different more positive thought, and move along."

I nod. I really do struggle with negative self-talk. It's going to take a lot more work to get through that.

"And Daniel?"

"Yeah?"

"You are doing an amazing job."

**May 23**

Graduation prep was something I had always looked forward to. It's the first stepping-stone out of this life into the next one. Now my stomach hurts thinking about it. I'm ready to be done with high school, but I'm not a hundred percent ready to figure out what I'm doing after that.

Here I am. Once class president, assumed valedictorian, soccer captain dropout, the big mighty epic fail, still not sure what I want to do with my life. And that's just fine.

-Daniel

I drag my feet into the school auditorium and up the bleachers. My heavy backpack drops with a thud. I have the excuse of finishing up three papers I'm still behind on, so I'm not planning on helping with grad set up. I pull out a notebook to work on an outline for my English final, and accidentally drop my pen and watch it roll off the seat and land under the bleachers somewhere. I stare at it for a minute. I should go get it. But I don't want to move. Instead I pull out another pen and start my outline.

"Hey, Daniel. Got a minute?" Shayla, our class's valedictorian sits next to me. Jace, the official salutatorian, stands a few rows below with his hands in his pockets.

Here we go again. "Sorry I'm not helping set up, I have some homework I need to catch up on before graduation." I grip my pen in my hand and push down the ping of jealousy that drops into my stomach.

"No, that's okay, we understand that. You've had a lot going on." Shayla sits up straighter. "I, well a bunch of us, from the student council, were wondering if you thought more about what we talked about a few days ago? That is if you want to, if you would maybe possibly..." She pauses and shifts on the bench.

"We want you to write a speech," Jace jumps in.

My hearing disappears for a moment and I swallow down the anxiety that rises in my throat. "I don't know."

Shayla clears her throat after glaring at Jace. "You're kind of an inspiration, with everything going on. And with you saving Garrett's life—"

"I didn't save his life. Get Garrett to do it. He was the one that almost died." I take in a deep breath to slow my heart down, but it doesn't help.

"He would have died if you weren't there," Jace speaks up.

Maybe there wouldn't have even been a car accident if I wasn't there.

"Look, I've been a jerk to you, I didn't really understand what was going on with you, and I'm sorry."

"You're an inspiration, Daniel, to a lot of us." Shayla shrugs. "I think it would be great if you wrote a speech. I mean if you want. You really don't have to." I can tell she's trying really hard not to bulldoze me.

An "inspiration." That word makes my stomach turn. I'm not an inspiration. How? How is having a breakdown and being taken to the hospital in front of the whole school inspirational? On second thought, maybe I'll skip graduation altogether. The school can mail me my diploma. I smile to myself. That's the first positive thought I've had all day.

"Just think about it. Please," Jace says.

Shayla nods in agreement.

"I don't know…" I accidentally drop my other pen and watch as it falls into the dark abyss below. Shit. Positive feeling gone.

"I got it." Jace runs to the bottom of the bleachers.

"No, leave it."

I watch as Jace jogs underneath the bleachers to pick it up, along with the other matching pen I dropped earlier, then back around and up the bleachers. "Here." He blows the dust off and holds them out to me.

I hesitate and stare at the pens, my hands already feeling thick and dry at the thought of touching them. It's just a feeling. I feel like they're contaminated, but they're fine. I feel like they're going to make me feel gross, but it's just a little dust, and that won't kill me. Still I say, "You can drop them in my bag." I pick up my backpack and pull it open for him. He drops them in and shoves his hands back in his pockets. I regret it instantly as I watch those two pens fall on top of the other pens and pencils at the bottom of the bag.

"Think about it," Shayla repeats. "But, could you email me by tonight with a yes or no, please? That would be helpful so we know what to do."

"Yeah. I'll let you know." If I remember my email password again.

"Don't stress about it. It's okay if you don't. But I think it would be cool if you did." Jace shrugs, and they both climb back down the bleachers.

Don't stress about it. I drop my notebook back in my bag and zip it up. I need bleach wipes for my pens before I can do my homework, so I make my way to Ms. Bender's classroom.

Maybe I'll work on my homework there too. It'll be much quieter than the gym. Positive feelings return.

## May 28

Today is the big day. My chest is so tight I'm afraid my bones are going to crumble from the pressure. Mom said as long as I remember to take my meds, and remember to breathe, I'll be fine. I will be fine. Anxiety is just a feeling. I won't die from it. But can I die from a full-fledged panic attack? I should look that up.

I still can't believe I said yes to Shayla and Jace. But I feel like it's something I have to do. My speech is ready, it's weird, maybe. But it's honest, and I'll be so glad when it's over. But I'm sure it'll be fine. Yeah, I'll be fine.

-Daniel

"This was a mistake. I can't go out there in front of all those people." I whisper under my breath and peek out from behind the heavy blue curtains that separate me from the rest of the world. Any positive thoughts or positive energy I tried to contrive have left me. Gone. Poof. Out some window somewhere.

"Why are you whispering?" Garrett whispers into my ear behind me.

I startle and nearly knock him over. "What are you doing here? Why aren't you in your seat?"

"Dude, you should feel the anxious vibe you put out. Everyone is getting twitchy out there."

"Shit." I tap my fingers across my sternum and take another step further away from the curtains.

"I would tell you to relax, but something tells me that would send you into a bigger spiral."

"It's great to know you're finally learning to listen to your conscience."

"Ha." He shoves my shoulder, but before I can grab my opposite shoulder, he shoves that one too and smiles.

The sound of my name floats from the stage and around the curtains.

Oh no. My heart sinks further into my shoes before packing its bags and racing out the backstage door. I clutch my speech to my chest and take a small step forward. I can do this. This is just a feeling, and sometimes feelings aren't reality. Except for this one. This is real. This speech is really happening. Okay, that feeling thing isn't really working right now.

"Come on, it's time." Garrett opens the curtain for me.

"I-I can't—" I change my mind and step back, out of the light from the stage. It hurts to breathe, a vice grip squeezes at my skull and I get dizzy.

They call my name again, followed by silence.

Principal Johnson sticks his head behind the curtain. "Daniel, that's your cue."

I nod, then shake my head. Why am I so nervous? I used to do stuff like this all the time. Where did my confidence go? I want it back.

Without missing a beat, Garrett snatches the paper from my hand. "I got this Mr. Johnson." His grin looks more like a grimace as he hobbles onto the stage before either of us can say anything.

"Are you okay?" Principal Johnson's confused question is drowned out by Garrett's stutters and the microphone feedback squeal.

"Hey, as you can see I'm not Daniel. I'm Garrett. But this is Daniel's speech. Most of you know, at least in our class know that Daniel had a hard time this year. And most of you fuckers turned your back on him."

"Garrett!" Principal Johnson breathes out from behind the curtain with me.

"Oh, yeah, sorry." He scratches his head and lets out a nervous laugh. "Well, anyways, I almost did the same, so reading his speech is the least that I can do." Garrett lets out a deep sigh and un-wrinkles the paper on the podium. "Wow, okay. Yeah. Again, Daniel wrote this." He clears his throat. "Confidence is a funny and fickle thing. One moment you can have all the confidence in the world, and the next, you're standing out in the middle of the street with no pants on. But in my case, it was Spanish class with no shirt. I only say that to take away the power my anxiety has had over me this whole year. I let my lack of confidence push people away. I let anxiety consume me. Sometimes I could control it, but most of the time, I couldn't.

"Our minds are also funny and fickle things. I've struggled with mine for as long as I can remember. By the time I hit junior high, I was able to keep most of my compulsions and ticks under control. Most of my friends thought my rituals were quirky, or that I was just 'a bit of a germaphobe' or a 'neat freak.' It felt so good to be 'normal' that I never spoke the letters OCD out loud for years. I even refused to let my own parents say it. I was embarrassed and ashamed to be labeled as different. I hated being OCD so much, I pretended it didn't exist. Not in my life.

"So, I tried hard to be just like everybody else. And things went well, for a while. I thought if I followed the rules, did what my parents asked, got good grades, did well in soccer, the OCD would just go away. That my parents would stay happy and stay together, that my best friend and girlfriend would never leave me. That I wouldn't be abandoned. That I could be normal.

"Normal is a funny and fickle word. Normal is what most people strive to be, but the rules are always changing and no one can ever keep up. Except for those who are making the rules. Normal is a word that we, I, have placed on top of a mountain of lies, allowing myself to believe that I will never be able to reach it. That it's something meant for other people who don't struggle like I do. Like others do. But normal looks different for everyone. And I think we all forget that sometimes. We can't judge others on what we think normal is based on our own lives. If we do, we will fail every time. And that was a hard lesson I had to learn this year. That I'm still learning.

"I have to constantly remind myself that my feelings don't always match up with reality. I felt like everyone thought I was a freak. So I blocked everyone out. I felt disgusting, so I had to shower so many times in a day. I felt like my parents, my dad didn't love me." Garrett pauses and takes in a deep breath.

"Feelings are funny and fickle things. Now that high school is over, we all have to go and find our confidence in new places. We have to discover what our new normals will look like, and we have to remember not to let our feelings get the best of us. It's a lesson I will have to constantly remind myself of. That's just my normal."

The auditorium is silent as Garrett clears his throat into the microphone. "We kind of failed Daniel this year. All of us. I really hope we all learn from his struggles and do better next time we see someone falling. None of us are immune, and no one wants to feel like they're all alone. I hope the class under us does a better job at taking care of each other. And maybe we'll all do a better job as we move on with our lives." He folds up the paper and makes his way back to his seat.

"Thank you," Principal Johnson says to me before he makes his way back out on the stage and starts clapping, encouraging everyone else to clap.

"Wow." I breathe out and step away from the curtain. That could have been worse. The nervous buzzing sensation leaves my body and floats towards the ceiling. I do feel like the final nail has been hammered into this coffin I call high school. I feel relieved. Bittersweet, but so much relief. A smile surprises me and spreads across my face.

Holy shit. I'm graduating.

## May 31

Today was my last therapy session with Dr. Hannah for the next four weeks. He's going on vacation with his family. It's weird to think he has a whole family of his own. I'm going to keep seeing him for a while I think.

He showed me where I can find some cognitive behavioral therapy papers online for some summer homework. I didn't realize that was so easy to find online.

I'm still struggling with my anxiety and with how my skin feels when I think I've touched something germ-infested, but I am feeling a bit more balanced. Dr. Hannah reminded me to stay on top of knocking down the negative thoughts, because they have a habit of sneaking back in when everything seems calm. But I'm not really worried about that. I feel safer knowing that I have my team backing me up.

-Daniel

## June 3

The house sold. Part of me wants to be really sad, but the other part of me is ready to leave this all behind. This house has been my anchor for as long as I can remember. I realize now it was my anchor because my parents were here, and they're leaving.

Mom apologized for being so absent. She took the divorce really hard. I was angry and confused with her about it too. She told me that she fell out of love and neither of them seemed to be able to connect again. Those words stung worse than I thought they would. The truth was a relief, but not in a soothing kind of way, but in a ripping-off-the-Band-Aid type of way, because somehow I still secretly felt like it was my fault.

I just want her to be happy.

-Daniel

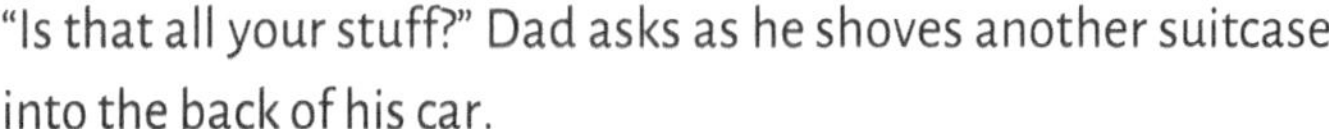

"Is that all your stuff?" Dad asks as he shoves another suitcase into the back of his car.

I nod and squeeze my arms around my waist. "It's weird. I thought I would be bringing my kids here one day."

"Yeah, me too." He places his hands on my shoulders and gives them a squeeze. "Your mom said she'll be back in the morning to finish cleaning up and to hand the keys over to the new owner."

My heart gives my chest one big bang to remind me of all the chapters closing in my life in the last few weeks.

"Hey, are you going to be okay?"

I shrug. Am I going to be okay? After my life completely dissolved this last year? After my parents divorced, I got dumped, and then had a very public mental breakdown? Do people really recover fully from all of that? I know I'm going to be fine. Dr. Hannah is helping me understand that there are going to be ups and downs. The OCD might be quiet for a while, and sometimes it'll be a loud resounding gong. But I have my support system. Not everyone has that, and for me, right now, that's enough. Am I going to be okay? "Eventually."

"Sometimes 'eventually' is the only answer you can give."

"I want to say 'yes.'"

"Me too. But I'm okay with eventually."

## June 10

I'm moved in with Dad in his new apartment for the summer, and Mom's traveling doing art shows. Everyone seems to be in a content place.

I'm excited about starting college with Garrett this fall. I'm ready to move on, but sometimes the thoughts still take over my brain and I get stuck in a loop. I've been working on telling Dad or Garrett when that happens so I don't spiral again. Doing the CBT papers Dr. Hannah gave me has been like rehab for my brain. I want to be able to control my mind again, not the other way around. It's a long process, I remember when I was younger I was in therapy for years to learn how to control my OCD. This feels very much like that. But this time I'm more experienced.

It's weird how people made a huge deal when I helped save Garrett's life, but not many people said anything about me saving my own life. Because I'm important too. I hate that I spent most of the year pushing people away and trying to fight on my own. But honestly, I didn't know what else to do.

I've been re-learning to fight for myself, and that's a powerful feeling. And I'm going to keep fighting, with my team by my side, because without them, I'm not sure if I would have survived this last year. I'm glad I did, because I'm not done yet.

-Daniel

www.rainn.org
(For help with sexual assault call: 1-800-656-4673)

www.thehotline.org
(For help with domestic abuse call: 1-800-799-7233)

www.doorofhope4teens.org
(Specializes in helping young adults
overcome self-harm and depression)

us.ditchthelabel.org

www.nami.org

d2lrevolution.com

www.thehopeline.com

www.ingramcontent.com/pod-product-compliance
Lightning Source LLC
Chambersburg PA
CBHW050346190726
48284CB00007BB/2169